TROPICAL BARTENDER BEAR

ZOE CHANT

SHIFTING SANDS RESORT

This book is part of a complete series, with recurring characters, but it does stand alone, with a satisfying happy-ever-after and no cliffhangers. Escape to Shifting Sands Resort and buckle up for a ten-book binge-read that will take you on a wild ride with a thrilling conclusion!

See also: the Shifting Sands Resort Omnibus, 4 volumes that include all the books, short stories, novellas, and three exclusive stories, all in the author's preferred reading order, available in ebook, paperback, audiobook, and hardcover!

PROLOGUE

FIVE YEARS AGO

*T*ex Williams met the eyes of the waiting customer and slid the beer glass expertly down the bar into his waiting hand. He tipped the brim of his hat and was unable to resist feeling like Tom Cruise in Cocktail when the customer gave him an enthusiastic thumbs up and the patrons between them applauded.

"Last call!" he hollered, in a voice that carried.

Then he turned to the gorgeous sepia-skinned woman who had just come in and staggered up to the bar. She was leaning heavily on it, wearing a tight, deeply-scooped magenta shirt and a short skirt. Knee-high, high-heeled boots completed the look.

"What can I get for you, ma'am?"

"Whiskey," she said boldly. "Neat. On the rocks."

Tex smiled indulgently at her. "Which one?"

She blinked back, confused. "Can't it be both?" she asked in a stage whisper, glancing at the next customer at the bar; she was packing up her purse and paying them no notice at all.

"Yes, ma'am," Tex replied in a matching whisper. Neat was a straight shot, on the rocks was over ice, so there was no way to do both. He turned to pour her a seltzer on ice with a twist of lime. "On the house," he said, not trying to swindle her.

She took it with no suspicion at all, gulping it down and shuddering as if she had just downed the strongest stuff that Tex had.

"You need me to call you a cab, honey?" Tex asked. He had a few cabbies that he trusted with cases like this on speed-dial.

The woman stared at him, clearly trying to make sense of his words.

"You got a friend here?" he asked gently.

"A friend?" She furrowed her brow, adorably trying to figure him out. Alarm passed over her face and she put a manicured hand to her mouth. "There was someone..." Her eyes widened. "Do you think that he could have put something in my drink?"

Tex was immediately on alert. No one was going to be slipping drugs to ridiculously innocent young women at his bar on *his* watch. He peered into her dark brown eyes, which were glassy, but not dilated. "What have you had to drink?" he asked her intently. "Did you ever leave your glass, to go to the bathroom? Who were you talking with?" His bear senses were at full strength—she smelled like hand soap and laundry detergent and leather and richly of alcohol, but not like drugs.

"I had some iced teas," she said, gazing back into his eyes trustingly. "Three Manhattan iced teas. Or New Jersey iced teas. Or something...?" she furrowed her brows again in that childlike way.

Tex relaxed. "Long Island iced teas?" he suggested. That matched the smell on her breath.

She tried to snap. "That was it!"

"You don't drink a lot, do you." Tex didn't make it a question.

She giggled and shook her head. "No."

She was a full-bodied woman, all her curves in just the right quantities for Tex's tastes. But if she wasn't used to drinking—which clearly she was not—three Long Island iced teas would explain her inebriation quite completely.

She was still trying to snap her fingers.

"What's your name?" Tex asked her, trying not to let his amusement show.

He needn't have worried; she was oblivious to anything but her disobedient fingers. "Jenny," she answered distantly. "Jenny Smith."

"I'm Tex." If she had been more sober, Tex might have guessed she was picking a generic fake name.

She must have realized that, as she raised sparkling eyes to him and added. "Well, it's really Jennavivianna Rose Smith. My parents didn't want me to have a boring name, and were devastated when I told them I'd rather be Jenny."

"You sit right here, Jennavivianna Rose," Tex told her, indicating a stool. "I'll make sure you don't pass out or do anything stupid. I'm going to give you a glass of water and a cup of coffee, and you put down whatever you can, you hear me?"

She gave a sloppy salute with a face-splitting grin as she clambered carefully up onto the barstool. "I trust you," she said. "I don't know why, but I trust you."

Tex poured the last few drinks for the other customers at his bar, keeping a careful eye on Jenny while she sipped her water and played with the bar napkin. The other customers gradually filed out as they finished their drinks and Tex failed to provide further inebriants. Tex wiped down the bar, and gathered up all the dirty dishes for the cleaning crew. The waitress began putting chairs upside down on tables and gave an old man nursing his last drink by the door a good-natured scold.

"How you doing, kitten?" Tex asked Jenny, wiping the counter around her. "Feel like being sick?" He'd been a bartender long enough to know the usual progression of a drunk that thorough.

She was clearly flagging as the alcohol wore slowly out of her system, but she shook her head firmly. "I don't usually drink," she confided. "This is all very out of character for me." Her gesture included her outfit and she pulled the shirt up at the shoulder self-consciously.

"You want to tell me about it?" The offer was automatic on Tex's part, but he meant it whole-heartedly.

Jenny looked at him with a hazy smile. "Yeah, I do. I mean I wouldn't usually, but hey, while we're being out of character, why not?"

Tex was pleased to see that her speech was clarifying. He was certain now that nothing was ailing her more than a bit too much to drink and he was able to shake off the vaguely guilty feeling that had been dogging him at the idea that someone could have slipped her something on his watch.

'It's not your bar,' he reminded himself. 'And you can't save every hard-luck case that comes through the door.'

She didn't look like a hard-luck case, though. Her hair was neatly trimmed, and her makeup was perfect. Her hands had the soft, subtly manicured look of someone who had gone through life without doing labor more menial than loading a dishwasher.

Even her voice as she spoke sounded educated. "It was my sister's idea," she confessed in a whisper, though the waitress was across the room closing things up well out of earshot.

"She thought you needed a night out on the town?" Tex gave her an encouraging smile.

Jenny rolled her eyes. "She thinks I'm a stick in the mud," she scoffed, forgetting to be quiet—or forgetting *how* to be quiet.

Tex wisely did not agree, but only made a sympathetic noise.

"She always has all the fun," Jenny complained. "I'm the responsible one, studying hard, scholarship to the University of Texas. She's so smart, she just skates by without working at all. She could be anything! She's so stylish and has so much fun." Her voice was full of affection and envy. "These are her clothes," she added wistfully.

"They look great on you," Tex told her sincerely. They certainly fit her just right.

"They look great on her," Jenny corrected him. "I look like a fraud. I feel like a fraud. I'm graduating in three months with a degree in law and I feel like I'm ready to panic and run away and do something crazy and reckless and throw it all away because I'm not as good as my grades say and who would even *let* me practice law and there's the bar and maybe someday I'll be a judge but that's just absolutely nuts and it's all just really overwhelming."

"It's pretty normal to feel like that," Tex assured her. "I've probably seen a hundred students in the last few months of their degrees who say variations of that. And it's okay to take a little break and be out of character and go out to a bar for a good time."

Jenny's look of relief was almost comical. Tex wondered how long she had been waiting for someone to say that to her.

"'Course, I have to say that because I work in a bar,"

he teased her, and was glad when she picked up that it was a joke and laughed richly.

"Did you go to college?" she asked, then backpedaled, "Sorry, that was probably too personal."

"Nah," Tex drawled easily back at her. "I never had the smarts for that. Thought I might make it as a musician, never really got further than amateur night and karaoke."

"I bet you sing really well. You have a great voice."

Tex wasn't sure if the warmth in her own voice was still the alcohol, or if she was flirting. "Thanks, sugar," seemed a safe enough reply.

"I'm leaving!" the waitress hollered, making true on her statement with a bang of the back door.

"Dreams are important," Jenny said firmly. "You shouldn't give up on being a musician."

"Dreams change," Tex said with a shrug. "I still like playing, but it's not a career I'd choose."

"What would you choose? Bartending?" From some people, it may have sounded condescending, but Jenny was genuine and naive; her question was sincere.

"Honestly, yes," Tex admitted. "I'd love to have my own place—maybe somewhere tropical."

"You ever seen…"

"Cocktail," Tex finished. "Yeah, I may have watched that at an impressionable age. Practiced juggling liquor bottles for hours to get it right."

Jenny sat up. "Let's see!"

Tex chuckled and picked two bottles from the counter. "Pro tip… full bottles have different balance than empty ones, and half-empty ones are worse. That lesson cost me half a paycheck when I dropped a 16 year old single malt."

He set the bottles easily in motion, spinning them in his hands and dipping them behind his back, even tossing one of them and catching it with a flourish.

Jenny squealed and clapped her hands appreciatively. "Oh my gosh, you have reflexes like a shifter!"

Startled, Tex fumbled the bottle, and then miraculously caught it before it hit the edge of the counter. Jenny's eyes went wide and she clapped her hand over her mouth. She met Tex's eyes and he knew that he had betrayed his understanding of the term with both his reaction and his reflexes.

"I mean... ah..." Jenny bit her lip. "I suppose we've eliminated the possibility that I was drugged into stupidity, but can I blame the iced teas for that slip?"

Tex had to laugh at her earnestness. "I hate to break it to you, but you're almost past that excuse, too."

Jenny gave a mortified groan.

"You're a shifter?" Tex asked. Somehow, she didn't fit into his expectation.

Jenny shook her head. "No, but otters and wolves run in my family. And I'm usually much better about being discreet about them."

Tex chuckled, replacing the bottles on the shelf. "Long Island iced teas can do that," he said understandingly.

"What's your animal?" she asked wistfully. "If you don't mind me asking."

"Bear," Tex said. "Brown bear."

"I didn't know there were brown bears in Texas," Jenny observed thoughtfully.

Tex leaned in. "Want to know a secret?"

Jenny nodded, eyes dancing.

"I was born in Oklahoma. And I don't admit that to just anyone."

Jenny laughed, an unlady-like snort of pure humor. "I can understand why."

Tex straightened up again. "Now you know all my secrets!"

"I won't tell a soul," Jenny promised. She rubbed her temples ruefully. "I don't think I will ever drink again, so I promise that this secret will be better kept."

"Circumstances were stacked against you," Tex drawled understandingly. "And anyway, it was part of the whole escape out of character."

Jenny cast her eyes down, giving a little half-smile. "It would be out of character for me not to go home alone, too," she suggested with an unexpected invitation.

Tex actually considered it. She was sober enough now that he trusted the offer was made with sound mind, and she was utterly, completely gorgeous, with warm brown eyes and dark, thick, shoulder-length brown hair. Her skin was a rich mahogany, the magenta shirt did little to hide the swell of perfect, overflowing breasts, and the tiny skirt hugged the sexiest hips Tex could imagine. In every way, she was everything he'd envisioned in his perfect mate. But something was holding him back, some sense that she wasn't quite right for him, and the only feelings she activated were protective.

"You don't want me, honey," he told her gently. "I'm unlucky in love. And I wouldn't want to be mixed up in the hangover you're going to have."

She looked disappointed, but accepting, and when Tex refilled her water glass, she gratefully drank it.

"Can I call you a cab?" Tex suggested gently.

This time Jenny nodded. "My sister was supposed to meet me here, but I'm guessing something came up with her job. I'll read her the riot act tomorrow, let me tell you."

She slipped off of her barstool to use the ladies room while Tex made the call, and he was pleased to see that her steps were no longer more wobbly than strange, high-heeled boots would indicate.

He finished cleaning the bar while she was busy, and

when she came out, the cab was already waiting at the curb.

Tex came around the bar to unlock the front door for her.

"Thanks," she said shyly, looking up at him with those beautiful brown eyes. "I feel like you came to my rescue tonight."

Tex tipped his hat at her. "Just doing my job, ma'am."

Jenny stretched up on her tiptoes and planted a chaste kiss on his stubbly cheek. "You're my hero," she told him.

Then she was slipping out the door for the cab, and Tex was locking the door behind her in bemusement. Somehow, he didn't think he'd seen the last of her.

CHAPTER 1

PRESENT DAY

*L*aurelangelina Smith woke in a hot panic, every one of her senses blazing, and she was out of bed and running into an unfamiliar wall before she remembered that she was not at her tiny condo, she was at Jenny's apartment, and... *Jenny*.

Laura reached for the odd psychic connection that she shared with her twin and found only emptiness.

Jenny was gone. There was no sense of her, anywhere that Laura could reach.

Still disoriented, Laura pulled one of Jenny's sensible bathrobes on and staggered out to the kitchen. Her head was pounding, but she knew that wasn't the reason that she'd woken up, or the reason that Jenny was so gone from her head.

You're an idiot, she railed at herself. *How could you have trusted those jerks? You knew better than to get mixed up in that scene.*

She expected a snarky response from her wolf, but only got wordless worry and grief in return.

Laura shuddered and opened the fridge. Nothing looked appetizing, and there was no Irish cream for her coffee. A drink, maybe a drink would calm the whirlwind in her head.

There was nothing more alcoholic in the cabinet than a rum fruitcake leftover from Christmas.

She nearly jumped out of the bathrobe when the phone on the table rang, and she was puzzled when her thumbprint didn't open it. Dammit. Jenny had grabbed the wrong phone on her way out, and left her own behind. The screen told her: Fred. Fred Kesser worked at the same firm that their father had worked at, where Jenny worked now. Trust Jenny's work to be calling at oh-god-hundred in the morning on a Monday.

Jenny...

Jenny was *gone*.

Laura buried her face in her hands and sank into a chair at the tiny table. She should *never* had sent Jenny to go shopping in her car. Had they blown it up? Sent a sniper? Shit. She never thought these things through.

Getting involved in the mob-like organization of the LA cartel had been so easy, so innocent. John had offered her good money at a tight time, and everything they asked for had been so simple and easy. In her small, gray wolf form, she could make discreet deliveries and pickups. She never saw what was in those little packages, never asked questions, never wanted to know.

But some part of her always knew, knew at least that it was bad news, and that she was being willful in her ignorance.

Then, finally she'd heard too much, seen too much, and she knew she couldn't continue.

Getting out was harder than getting in, of course.

She swallowed to remember Blacksmith's eyes, and his threat. "You tell anyone about this, and shifting won't save you."

And now Jenny, *Jenny* was *gone* and there was no *way* it wasn't related.

Laura hadn't smoked a cigarette in two years now, and she had never wanted one so badly.

Hours later, when the cops finally knocked on the door, she had still not found anything to drink.

"Ma'am, are you Jennavivianna Smith?"

Laura blinked. "Jenny," she said weakly. Jenny hated her full name.

"Ma'am, I'm afraid there's been an accident. Your sister's car was just pulled out of the water by Handle's Curve."

Laura gripped the door frame tighter. They'd probably cut the brake lines, or tampered with the steering or something. In the dark, in the spring rain... and Jenny wasn't as good at driving as Laura was—she commuted by bus or train and didn't even own a car.

"No body has been found, yet. The search is ongoing."

Then it hit her. They thought that *she* had gone off the road. They thought that Jenny was standing here, and that her hapless, screw-up sister Laura was the one who had died. Laura gave a little moan of pain.

The second cop reached out a hand to her and offered words of sympathy and support that Laura brushed off, not even hearing over the buzzing in her head.

"Yes, thank you. I'll be okay. I've got... friends, yes. I'll be okay. Yes, please keep me updated." She brushed them off as best as she could, going through the puppet-motions as she imagined Jenny might.

They didn't say a word that implied they might think it

wasn't an accident and Laura said nothing to suggest it, either.

When she'd finally shut the door behind them, she leaned against it for a long moment. It had all been one long lie, from 'I'll be okay' to 'Thank you.' But it had been easier than she guessed to put herself in Jenny's shoes.

Jenny's phone showed a voicemail alert. Laura unlocked it with the code they'd used for bike locks when they were little and listened to it.

"Marty thinks you should go to Costa Rica to represent the firm," Fred said after a brief opening ramble about contracts and files. "You're the one who got the old contract annulled and the new one ready in time. And you're totally due a break. Give it some thought, and find your passport. The World Mr. Shifter finals are just next week, so we've got to make the airline reservations right away."

It was one of the few things that the sisters had in common—a weakness for ridiculous pageants. Mostly, it meant snarking together over pints of ice cream on the couch. A shifter pageant—was it just a gimmick, or was it actually a male beauty contest for shifters? And Costa Rica… she had always dreamed of going there.

It suddenly occurred to Laura that Costa Rica was more than just a tropical destination—it could be her escape. She wouldn't be able to maintain the facade of Jenny's life very long; she could fit what she knew about contract law in a pen cap with room leftover. But she could start a new life in a foreign country where no one knew either of them.

It didn't take Laura more than a few moments to find Jenny's passport—the whole apartment was ridiculously tidy and well-organized, and passports and important cards were thoughtfully filed at her desk. The same passcode that had opened her phone unlocked her laptop, but Laura couldn't bear to look through it.

With a deep breath, Laura called Fred back.

She didn't have to feign the tears that came as she explained why she wouldn't be in to work. "My sister... there was an accident." *It was my fault*, she didn't say. *And it wasn't an accident.*

Fred fell all over himself trying to comfort her as she choked out the parts of the story that she could.

"No, of course you don't need to come in. We'll give your cases to Julie, naturally. Don't feel bad, take whatever time you need."

Painfully glad that Fred had not pressed her with any details about those cases, Laura hesitantly said, "The... the Mr. Shifter contest—"

"You wouldn't have to go, of course," Fred said quickly, then seemed to stumble and reconsider. "But you could, if getting away sounds good. You know, a change of scenery. While you... ah... recover."

As if she could ever *recover* from this. The best Laura could hope for was *escape* from this. "A change of scenery sounds good," Laura saved him gratefully.

"I'll get Marty to put everything in order," Fred assured her. "We'll get you the tickets right away, send you the itinerary. Do whatever you need to do."

"Thanks Fred," Laura said sincerely. She tried not to think about how poorly she would be thanking him, abandoning Jenny's job and fleeing the country altogether.

"Anything you need," Fred repeated. "Anything you need, you let me know."

"I will," Laura lied. *I need my sister.*

She pulled out her wallet after she hung up and stared at the photo on her license.

The face—her face and Jenny's—was so familiar. The

name wasn't hers anymore. Jenny's hefty kitchen shears split the photograph, and the shreds of the card were cast into the garbage disposal. Laura's credit card, already maxed out anyway, followed swiftly. Jenny's passport would get her out of here, and she had enough information and identification to access her accounts through her laptop.

Even dead, Jenny was saving her butt.

CHAPTER 2

$\mathcal{T}$he conference room behind the restaurant was stuffed to the seams. Tex wryly thought that if they were going to keep adding staff members, they would have to start meeting in the grand event hall where they held exercise classes and weekly formal dances.

Tex chivalrously stood when a strange woman in the Shifting Sands housekeeping uniform edged into the room and glanced around for a chair.

"Merci!" she said sweetly, with a grateful smile. She sank gracefully into the offered chair.

"Too bad we don't have new French maid uniforms to go with the new French maids," Breck, the headwaiter, hissed near his ear appreciatively as Tex backed up to the wall with folded arms.

"I think she's French Canadian," Tex whispered back. She smelled like too much perfume.

Not that Breck would care where she was from. Breck appreciated all women, and all men, for that matter.

When Scarlet entered, the chatter died to a murmur and then turned into an attentive silence at her frown.

"As you know, we've got a lot of new staff to welcome," she said briskly. "We aren't in preschool, so we aren't going to go around the room and introduce ourselves, but do take a moment to look around and see who's new and make a point of saying hello to those you don't know. On your own time." Her green eyes traveled appraisingly across the room and Tex met them briefly.

"The World Mr. Shifter finals will officially begin one week from today, but we'll be getting new guests every day between now and then, and they'll be doing a lot of the early interviews and photoshoots starting in two days. Travis?"

Travis, a lynx shifter from Alaska who was in charge of repairs and maintenance, looked like he hadn't gotten sleep in several days. The impression was probably accurate; he had been pulling all-nighters since the resort had gotten the news about the event's last-minute change of venue, desperate to get enough of the housing into shape to house the influx.

"All of the primary cottages are ready for occupancy, and the hotel has been brought back up to code. The hot water in the west wing isn't working yet, but should be by tonight. The toilets..."

Tex let Travis' report flow over him as he assessed the new staff. There were at least half a dozen new house-keeping staff, two new kitchen assistants, two new waitstaff who would split time between the dining hall and Tex's pooltop bar, a green-looking carpenter to work with Travis, and a second lifeguard to relieve Bastian. Even Graham, the standoffish lion shifter in charge of landscaping, had been assigned a new helper, though Graham had already made it clear the young man would be doing nothing but the most basic tasks, like lawn-mowing and hauling clip-pings. Tex suspected that he found the whole idea of an assistant deeply offensive, and the gardens had gone from immaculate to some new state of perfection, even while the gardener cleared vast new swathes of jungle encroachment back from the cottages that were being put back into use and tamed it into hedges of flowers and thick leaves.

"You want us to move?" Bastian said unexpectedly, in response to something Travis said.

Tex turned his wandering attention back to Travis, who squirmed and looked guilty, glancing at Scarlet for support.

"It's not that we'd have to," he said defensively. "It's just that the houses on the south cliffs are set up as a large private family manors, never made for individual rentals. It would take a lot of work to convert them into private rooms, and they'd be a hard sell the way they're configured now, with shared bathrooms and living space. But they're in fine working condition, and if the staff moved to those three houses, we'd free up twenty more rooms in the hotel."

Scarlet was nodding, paying no mind to Bastian's disgruntled muttering about sharing a bathroom. "Let's make this happen. I understand that it's not ideal," the withering look she gave Bastian was as much sympathy as he could expect out of her, "but our waiting list has never been this long, and this is a chance we can't let escape us."

She glanced around the room. "Chef?"

"Travis has the new freezer working," the distinguished older man reported, "and it's fully stocked. Our supplier on the mainland says there should be no problem filling the orders we've put in for the next few weeks, and I've got everything that can be made ahead ready to go." He nodded at his new assistants. "I'm confident my team and I can get you meals that will do the resort proud."

He earned the tiniest hint of smile from Scarlet. "I'm glad to hear that. We'll need to coordinate an extra trip to the mainland mid-week, from the looks of the order forms, but that shouldn't be problematic. Tex?"

Tex sat up straighter. "We're well-stocked in everything hard, but the white wine shipment came in four cases short."

Scarlet frowned. "Four cases?"

"I counted twice," Tex assured her.

"I'll call and have words with the distributor," Scarlet said, and Tex was glad that he wouldn't be on the receiving end of that call. "We may need to pick some up on the mainland if they can't get the replacement here by next week."

"We'll have a better idea of how well stock is holding up pretty quickly," Tex agreed. "Maybe they'll all be red wine drinkers. Incidentals are in good order, plenty of napkins and tiny umbrellas, and the fruit shipment exceeded my expectations this week."

Scarlet continued through housekeeping, and then got a thumbs up from Lydia, the black swan shifter who managed the spa. Other than a few minor supply concerns, and Travis' warning about overtaxing the septic system, they seemed ready for the oncoming crowd. Scarlet seemed cautiously optimistic.

"I'm really pleased with how well you've all stepped up and gotten everything together," she told them candidly, and Tex was as surprised as he was proud; Scarlet was notoriously stingy with her praise.

"We've got a busy few weeks ahead of us and I know you'll be asked to do more than usually do. It's going to be crowded and we're all going to be under a lot of scrutiny. I trust you can handle it, and that we will make this a *pleasantly* memorable event. Go make it happen."

The meeting broke up with high energy and cheer.

Breck immediately introduced himself to the new French-speaking housekeeper.

As Tex slipped out past Scarlet, she took him aside. "I haven't seen Gizelle in a while." It wasn't quite an accusation.

"She's still not good with crowds, ma'am," Tex said apologetically.

Scarlet nodded thoughtfully. "She's going to have a rough few weeks," she said pityingly.

"I think we all may," Tex said candidly, earning a dry laugh from Scarlet.

Except for the extra staff, Shifting Sands didn't look any different. It still had that peculiar poised energy that Tex thought was due to the way the sun glittered off the white tiled decks and retaining walls. Photographers were already on site, taking light readings and doing test shots of the dramatic pool steps.

Gizelle was sitting behind the bar polishing silverware that was already clean, her salt-and-pepper hair obscuring her face. She scrubbed at each fork with a corner of her sundress, then held it up to the light critically. "Not much of a hoard," she said critically, when Tex found her.

"I'm not a dragon," he reminded her gently. "I'm a bear. Bastian is the dragon."

"Bastian doesn't think he is a good dragon," Gizelle said airily.

"Scarlet noticed that she hasn't seen you around in a while," Tex told her, crouching down and taking the basket of forks that she handed him.

"Scarlet notices things," Gizelle agreed, unconcerned. "She notices the sky with no sun."

"There's going to be a lot of people coming here in the next few days," Tex warned her. They'd talked about the upcoming Mr. Shifter event several times, but he wasn't really sure how much of it made sense to her.

As far as anyone could tell, Gizelle had spent her entire childhood as a gazelle, a captive in the zoo of a sadistic shifter collector. She didn't know her own name, or have any memory of parents or human shape before coming to Shifting Sands. She could have been twenty-five, or fifty; the white streaking her dark hair made her look ancient, but her face was unlined and innocent. She had a tendency to flee at the slightest hint of conflict, shifting into her gazelle shape and leaping high into the air. There had been several times Tex wasn't sure how she avoided breaking one of her fragile-looking legs as she landed.

Gizelle looked up at him, big eyes behind her wild, loose hair. "I know," she said reluctantly. "Too many people are coming, so *loud*, and there will be photographers to avoid. But I'll still help. Graham lets me rake sometimes, and Chef lets me wash the dishes. I broke a glass, to see how it would sound, but he told me I could still do the silverware."

Tex ruffled her hair gently, a privilege she didn't allow everyone. "You'll be fine. You want to go help Graham with that raking?"

She nodded with a slow grin and stood up, padding silently away on dirty, bare feet.

As Tex was giving the basket of forks a quick sift for anything unexpected, she popped back into the bar and warned him, "Some of the people are going to be bad. Listen through your nose!"

Then she vanished again.

CHAPTER 3

*S*hifting Sands was everything the brochure promised, Laura thought, looking down at it from the entrance.

Cottage roofs scattered through jungle greenery stepped down the hill before her, dipping down to a gorgeous crescent beach and a shimmering green ocean, waves lapping invitingly, even from this vantage. A few bigger buildings were artistically arranged to the south and an enormous pool gleamed from a white tiled deck.

The grounds were lush shades of green with riotous flowers everywhere providing spots of color and a distinct, dreamy scent.

"Excuse me," an impatient accented voice said behind her, and before she could move, she was being elbowed aside by a man carrying a suitcase whose bland white suit did nothing to hide the fact that he was clearly a bodyguard.

"Excuse *me*," Laura snapped, moving back inside the entrance. It was a little more crowded than the brochure had suggested. The courtyard was filled with people waiting to check in, and heaps of suitcases and travel bags lined the walls. They were clustered in groups—little flocks of attendants for each of the Mr. Shifter candidates, with their dark glasses and celebrity expectations.

"We'll need fresh linens every day, of course." The woman's American accent was strident and demanding.

"Of course! We'll do everything possible to make your stay pleasant and memorable." Laura recognized the clerk's silky, Spanish-accented tone at once. She'd worked in hospitality before; that was the 'your coffee will be spit into twice daily, but I'm going to smile' voice.

Beside the American woman, a man was leaning on the counter. He was definitely one of the Mr. Shifter contestants, his shirt unbuttoned halfway showed plenty of tanned pecs and he caught Laura's glance to give her an overly white-toothed, leering grin.

"We'll need breakfast delivered promptly at 9 each morning," his assistant continued.

"I'm sorry ma'am, food is only served at the restaurant. It is open 24 hours with a limited self-serve buffet, and has regular meals at..."

"There's no room service?" Her voice raised a scale. "What kind of fly-by-night resort is this?"

The clerk's voice remained steady. "I think you'll find the breakfasts our chef makes are worth the early trip," she said cheerfully.

"What are the bar hours?" the Mr. Shifter contestant asked in a lazy Californian accent. That clinched Laura's guess that this was the American representation and she was already embarrassed for her country.

"Wine and beer are available in coolers at all hours, the staffed bar is open until midnight each night." The woman pushed their keys over the counter with a pamphlet. "You're in cottage eight, here is a map that shows you the way; your cottage is circled in red. There's a schedule of events listed here."

"You don't have anything closer to the beach?" It was half whine, half kissing up, in a lightning fast swap of attitude as the assistant realized that she might need leverage with the clerk.

Laura was impressed by the clerk's sweet, even response. "I'm sorry, we're booked solid for the next week."

"Well, I suppose it will have to do, then."

From her tone, Laura could already imagine the Yelp review that the American assistant was composing in her head. 'Resort was not able to accommodate my many and ridiculous demands. Terrible service. Spotted several insects. Staff in foreign country had actual accents.'

She was smirking over the idea in her head when Mr. America caught her eye again and he seemed to think her smile was about him. He winked, and Laura could feel the smile on her face freeze and turn brittle.

She was done with men. Pretty faces and nice muscles and her own destructive attraction to self-centered jerks had gotten Laura into this mess in the first place.

She wasn't going to make all those same mistakes again.

She scowled back and Mr. America looked surprised. She stalked back to her modest pile of luggage and waited while his assistant fussed about having their bags delivered and kvetched about how far it was to walk and how steep it looked. She admired the courtyard instead, with its lovely planters full of exotic things. Green vines draped down in veils from the center of the open yard, and the indirect light was gorgeous and otherworldly.

The Americans finally left, and two sets of Asian contingencies checked in. These, too, were clearly Mr. Shifter contestants with their assistants and a bodyguard apiece. The one that Laura guessed was Mr. China did his own registration, an assistant and an older man who may have been a trainer or a bodyguard waiting behind him. The other let his cheerfully forward assistant handle everything while he smiled and nodded a lot.

The last one before Laura in line was an eastern European man with incredibly green eyes and thick dark hair. A tropical white shirt did nothing to hide his incredible physique. He waited haughtily across the room with their luggage reading his phone while his secretary tripped across the room to complete their registration. She was uselessly giggly, had lost the confirmation number, and it took several extra moments while she fumbled for the correct credit card.

"I'm sorry it's taken so long," the woman behind the counter said with her lilting Spanish accent when Laura was finally able to approach. Her nametag said "Lydia."

"No worries," Laura said warmly, giving a wry smile of understanding. "You've had your hands full. Jenny Smith."

Lydia's professional smile became more real. "Do you have your confirmation number?"

Laura had used her copious waiting time to find her numbers and get Jenny's credit card, and she gave them both to Lydia.

"Perfect," Lydia said gratefully. "We've got you in the hotel, room 320 on the top floor." She said it neutrally, probably knowing how it sounded after the fancy cottage assignments she'd given to the Mr. Shifters before her.

"That sounds great," Laura said genuinely.

Her pamphlet had a map of the resort with the narrow hotel building circled. "You'll want to use the second door," Lydia said, indicating it on the map with a little blue dot. "And go ahead and use the staff elevator, it's directly on your left when you go in. Ignore the sign;

there's no keycard required for it." She gave Laura a warm wink.

"Thanks," Laura said, and they shared a companionable smile.

"I've got a sunrise yoga class in the event hall if you're up." Lydia added shyly, pointing to the schedule on the back of the pamphlet.

Laura's smile slipped; sunrise and Laura didn't really get along, but she knew that Jenny was an early riser. And if she was going to maintain the charade... "I'll... try to wake up in time."

"Jetlag can be a drag," Lydia said kindly. "You'll be welcome if you can make it."

"Thanks," Laura said weakly. Jenny had been dedicated if not enthusiastic about her yoga classes, even if her efforts hadn't given her a shape any different than her lazier twin sister's.

Laura took her key and turned back to her bags. At first, she thought it was another Mr. Shifter contestant who was stalking up; he certainly had that Mr. Shifter physique. Then he started to take her bags, and Laura recognized that he was wearing a staff polo shirt with a nametag: Graham.

"I've got these," she said, before he could pick them up. "They stack, and have wheels, so I'm fine."

He grunted and shrugged, and went to fetch another pile of luggage without so much as a sideways glance. He picked up half the pile without a hint of effort and left as abruptly as he'd come in, festooned with bags.

Well, that one wouldn't have gotten far through the personality competition, Laura thought wryly. She slung her purse over her shoulder and just as she was about take her bags and find her hotel room, she heard, "Jenny! Jenny!"

It was a heartbeat before Laura remembered that she *was* Jenny, and she turned with a resigned sigh to smile and wave weakly at Fred as he came in with the next surge of guests in the single courtesy van from the tiny airport.

It had just become a dozen times more difficult to maintain her cover.

CHAPTER 4

A scream broke the hot afternoon lull. Tex dropped the drink he was making and vaulted over his counter without a second thought, bringing the baseball bat he kept there automatically. It was a short sprint out the back door and he spent those strides wondering what insane threat to expect this time.

For such a quiet little resort, Shifting Sands got some strange events. In the months that Tex had been working there, there had been a hostage situation with South American mercenaries, someone had wired the resort generators to blow up, and a crazy rare shifter collector had been kidnapping guests. Once, he'd had to break up a lion and bear fight. What would it be this time, the mob?

No, no, he told himself, this was Central America, probably it was the *cartel* here.

Graham materialized from a hedge with a machete just as Tex made the back entrance of the bar. There they found the new maid with the French accent standing on the sidewalk, clutching her armful of fresh folded towels and shrieking at the top of her lungs. A wide column of ants was making their merry way across her path and she was backing up from them in horror.

Graham lowered his machete, gave her a dirty look, and vanished back into his beloved greenery. The few guests who had followed him to discover the source of the commotion decided there was nothing to see and returned to the bar, grousing about dramatics.

Feeling as sorry for Graham's disgusted look as he did for the ants, Tex leaned his baseball bat against the doorframe and crossed the ants with one extra long stride.

"Don't worry, ma'am. They occasionally get it in their little ant heads to march from some place to some other place, but they'll be done in no time at all. It's the jungle, after all, you've got to expect some insect encroachers. Graham does his best to keep them off most of the paths, but there's a limit to what even he can do."

The maid—her nametag said Marie, which was just perfect—threw herself into Tex's arms, towels and all.

"There's so *many* of them!" she sobbed. Her French accent was strangely gone.

Tex looked at the ants in some bewilderment. He'd gotten used to them, and suspected that Marie would not last long at Shifting Sands if she wasn't able to handle a simple ant migration. "You should see what happens to the cottages if people sneak food back to them," he said, patting her on the shoulder and hoping that the humor was reassuring.

She continued to sob on him.

"Now there, it's okay. You can just step right over them, they won't even notice you."

She made a noise of alarm and clung to him harder.

"Alright, then, ma'am, hold on."

She was barely an armful, even heaped with towels, and Tex was able to swing her up and carry her over the offending column of ants. He set her down on her feet, but she continued to hold on, clutching the towels between them.

"You're safe, ma'am," he said, slightly strangled. "You can let go now."

It took a more obvious effort to pry her off before she released him. "*Mon dieu*," she said, wiping at her eyes. "You are my hero."

Tex wondered if he'd imagined her French accent vanishing, it was certainly thick enough now. He tipped his hat at her. "It's the least I can do, ma'am."

Marie gave a little moan. "Oh, *mes serviettes*!" she said, shaking her head at her rumpled armful.

"Your… oh, your towels? They haven't suffered any," Tex reassured her. "I'll help you fold them and no one will know a thing about their brush with the army of *formicidae*."

She furrowed her brow at Tex adorably, and he smiled at her. "Ants," he explained. "Just ants."

Her face brightened in understanding, and Tex helped her shake the towels back into presentable shape and fold them neatly into squares again.

"My hero," she repeated, and the look she shot back over her shoulder as she trotted away down the clear trail to the cottages suggested that she was willing to reward Tex's chivalry.

Tex wasn't sure why the offer was so unappealing. She was a good-looking woman, with very definite charms. Dating within the housekeeping pool didn't offend Tex's good sense about not seeing coworkers; he would never had been even tempted by someone who worked the bar with him. But although he appreciated the view as she walked away with a little extra swing in her hips, he didn't find himself wanting to chase her down.

It wasn't just that he felt the weight of his bad luck in love, he felt like he was… waiting for something.

With a shrug, he collected his baseball bat and returned to the bar. Dropping the drink had not broken the glass, but there was a mess of spilled syrup to clean up, and an impatient crowd of guests had gathered while he was away.

"Sorry folks," he said, swiftly stepping up to give the mess a brief swab. "A lady screams, you've got to be ready to drop things and run to the rescue," he said smoothly. He added a wink for one of the older ladies at the counter, and was repaid by watching her grouchy expression turn to a delighted blush.

"What can I get for you?" he asked the first person at the bar. He got all their requests while he remade the interrupted drink.

They were all duly impressed when he could remember what each of them had asked for without pausing to write anything down, serving even the most meticulously-ordered drink exactly as dictated. He spun a bottle on each hand as a finishing touch, and got a scattered round of applause from the ones who had remained at the counter to see the whole show.

"I'll take a Shifter's Mate," a familiar voice said from the end of the counter as the others dispersed. A sunhat and a wave of dark hair obscured her face as she bent over the laminated drink menu, shoulders slumped. She lacked the manic energy that the rest of the resort seemed to have right now.

"Coming up, ma'am," Tex said automatically, trying to place the voice and figure out why it was giving him such an unexpected electric thrill. He dropped the ingredients into the shaker with a few cubes of ice and shook it efficiently while he filled a glass with clean cubes in the other hand. An umbrella and a wedge of fruit at the rim finished his own invention.

"Pretty," the woman said, finally looking up.

"P-p-pretty," he echoed her, unable to come up with anything more. He remembered that face and those brown eyes, but that last time he had seen her had been nothing like this.

She is ours, his bear roared gleefully.

Jennavivianna had been gorgeous then, but now she was something infinitely more. Every curve of her body was an invitation, every wave of her dark hair was a promise. The planes of her lovely face were perfectly composed and the eyes—those limitless, bottomless, aching eyes! A man could drown in those places, if he let himself go.

And Tex was ready to jump.

CHAPTER 5

It would be a short and easy trip to become a drunk in the wake of her sister's murder, Laura thought, but she knew she needed her wits about her. She had hoped that Shifting Sands would be a safe escape from anyone who knew Jenny, the perfect place to springboard a new life in a foreign country. The resort had people from all over the globe and she planned to make use of her time to get to know some of them, maybe even get a lead for work that wasn't too careful about looking at visas. It didn't have to be in Costa Rica, she could get her return ticket changed to anywhere!

But she hadn't planned on Fred.

Fred had decided to join her at the last minute and, while he was fortunately not able to get all the same flights as Laura, he was staying at the hotel just a few doors down.

"I didn't like the idea of you off in some foreign place so soon after the loss of your sister," he said, so earnestly that it was impossible to hate him for fouling up her strategy so completely. "Isn't it lucky they were able to open up a few new rooms?"

It was only lucky if you counted *bad* luck.

Now, instead of planning her escape in two weeks, Laura was agonizing over everything she said and did—did she say that like Jenny would have? Was she walking like Jenny did? She chose to wear the modest one-piece that Jenny would have, though she'd been surprised to find a sky blue bikini in her sister's closet. She even kept a sensible hat on, though her brown skin wouldn't burn. She had used jetlag and headaches as excuses for avoiding Fred at meals so far, but she knew that wouldn't last long. She was dreading the time when he'd finally try to talk work with her, and she'd have to stare at him blankly.

He was such a nice guy and he'd been such a good friend to Jenny and their parents over the years that Laura felt awful for brushing him off so coldly. She consoled herself by thinking that he would probably assume her chilly behavior was because she was grieving.

Her grief felt oddly far away. She couldn't really believe that Jenny was gone. They still hadn't found a body by the time she'd left Los Angeles, but there was no way she could have survived the crash or the ocean... was there? The police had given her no reason to hope. But it still wasn't *real* that she'd died. Despite the silence of their psychic bond, Laura couldn't help but expect her just to walk into the bar and scold her for slouching.

She felt restless, but she didn't think that's what grief ought to feel like.

She scanned the laminated drink menu, trying to decide which one Jenny would pick.

"I'll take a Shifter's Mate," she called to the bartender who'd been showing off at the other end of the counter without looking. It called itself a 'Shifting Sands original, a Mai Tai with a Costa Rican twist.' It would be like Jenny to take a fruity house specialty and it would undoubtedly be mostly cheap juice and a plastic sword.

She only watched the bartender's ridiculous drink-making out of the corner of one eye, not lifting her hat until he set the drink before her.

"Pretty," she had to admit, and then she made the mistake of looking him in the face.

He was as handsome as any of the Mr. Shifters, with a tan and build that Mr. California himself would envy. His easy smile was not as fakely white, and his hands were both strong and gentle on the glass he hadn't let go of. He was wearing a cowboy hat, of all the ridiculous things. Laura had no patience for the pretentiousness of cowboys and hated their music.

She wanted to dislike him at once but, instead, she was utterly drawn to him. His brown eyes had crinkles of kind-ness and humor around them and Laura had never wanted to touch a jaw as much as she wanted to touch his. The almost-scruffy stubble, the straight nose, and the stunned look—he was straight off a Western romance book cover.

"P-p-pretty," he echoed her.

Laura wondered if he was as stunned as she felt, or if he was just an idiot. Being an idiot would simplify things, at least.

He's not an idiot, he's ours, her wolf told her firmly, canine voice singing in delight.

He blinked and shook his head, which gave her just enough space to do the same.

"You're Jenny," he said, to Laura's shock. "Jennavi-vianna Rose."

Laura had no words. She'd come halfway around the world to escape her life, just to meet a bartender who knew her *sister*?

"We met in Austin, half a dozen years ago. Over spring break." He sounded baffled.

"Oh wait, yes!" Laura blurted. Jenny had told her about this, when she returned her borrowed boots. "You were very kind to her—to ME. You were really sweet. To me."

Ours, not hers, her wolf said jealously.

"Can I get you something?"

Laura barely avoided asking him to take his pants off and make love to her right there in the crowded bar. "You, ah, already took my order," she reminded him. "You're still holding onto it."

He gave a confused guffaw and let go of the glass. His fingers left bare spots in the gathering drops of condensation. Laura put her own fingers there and wondered if she imagined the little electric shock it gave her.

She knew what this was from the stories and from her inner wolf's animal glee. She'd never really believed she'd find her own mate, but she knew it was possible. Love at first sight, it was supposed to be. Like this, except not complicated by the fact that she was masquerading as someone else. Someone he'd already met.

She concentrated on his cowboy hat and worked at keeping her expression blank and casual. It was something she had a lot of practice with lately; act stupid, keep her head down, try not to put too much together.

"Can I get *you* something?" she asked, chilling her voice deliberately.

He actually blushed as he realized he was staring at her. It was one of the most adorable things she'd ever seen. He put his fingers to his hat in a gesture that could only be automatic. "I'm sorry, ma'am," he said humbly. "It's… ah… a surprise to see you again."

"It was a long time ago," Laura agreed with a careless

shrug. It was tricky pretending disinterest when everything about him made her heart race and her breath catch. "Small world."

'He's a cowboy,' she reminded herself. 'You *hate* country music.'

She clung to that and took a sip of the drink.

He was still staring at her.

For the first time on the trip, she was actually glad to hear Fred's voice. "There you are, Jenny!"

She turned with a warm smile for the bartender's benefit and a little wave. "Hey Fred."

Fred plopped down beside her on a barstool, completely innocuous and out-classed in his flip-flops and sunburnt balding head.

The bartender's face, when she snuck a look, was a hilarious mixture of jealousy and confusion. Laura might have laughed out loud under different circumstances. "This is Fred," she introduced casually. "We work together." She wasn't actually that sure where in the hierarchy of the law office Fred fell, or for that matter, what Jenny's exact position was, which did nothing but complicate her acting efforts.

The bartender tipped his hat automatically to Fred. "Pleased to meet you," he drawled. "I'm Tex."

Of *course* he was. Laura had to keep her eyes from rolling.

"We met a few years back when I was in Austin for spring break," Laura offered.

Fred extended a sweaty hand for a handshake. "Did you go to college down there?"

Tex looked abashed. "No, sir. I'm not a college man. I've been a bartender since the law let me."

"Nothing wrong with that," Laura snapped in his defense before she could stop herself. She'd never managed more than a semester or two of college herself and Tex's embarrassed look hit her in several ways.

"Of course not," Fred said jovially. "It's not for everyone."

Laura gritted her teeth as his patronizing tone, but couldn't say anything. She was supposed to be Jenny, who'd done seven or eight years of higher education, so she shrugged and took a sip of her drink, nearly stabbing herself in the cheek with the stupid umbrella.

She let Fred and Tex fumble through a conversation without her, sipping at her drink like it would save her. A "Shifter's Mate," it was called, and just like the real thing, it was sweet, with a kick of intoxication and a twist of sour.

Her mate. She'd found her mate.

Our mate, her wolf corrected, practically purring in her ear. She, for some reason, did not seem to consider the cowboy hat a deal breaker. Nor did she mind that Tex was a bear, something that they both seemed to instinctively know.

These things don't matter, her wolf said dismissively.

How about the fact that we're masquerading as our twin sister and he's already met her. That might confuse the issue.

Aren't you humans used to confusion by now? You certainly seem to thrive on it.

Sometimes Laura felt like Jenny was the lucky one, not being a shifter.

She caught herself watching Tex out of the corner of her eye. He was telling Fred his choices of high end gin for a gin and tonic. Fred was trying to look knowledgeable about the selection.

Laura emptied her drink, wishing it had been four times as strong, and ate the fruit off the umbrella stick. "I have to use the ladies," she said, hopping down off her barstool. Fred would probably wait here for an hour or more before he figured out she wasn't coming back.

"Wait," Tex said too loudly. Other patrons of the bar turned to look curiously, and a pause in the tinny Spanish radio music gave the moment a surreal edge.

Laura turned back, and gave what she hoped was a cool stare back at him.

"I'm pretty sure I don't have to pay," she said dryly. "This place is supposed to be all-inclusive."

"No, of course, it's just..."

He was adorable, fumbling through his obvious confusion. Laura could not get over how expressive his mouth was, or how perfect the line of his jaw was. She'd been turned on by men before, but none of them had ever made her as literally weak in the knees as this. Between the tropical heat and the sanity-eating lust this man was igniting in her, she thought she actually understood why heroines in dirty novels sometimes swooned.

"Can I see you, later?" he finally stammered.

She wanted to say yes. She honestly didn't want to leave his presence; every move away from him felt like betrayal.

But he was a complication in a plan already made painfully complex by Fred. A mate wasn't a mandate and she was past the point in her life where she let her loins lead her around.

"I'm not interested," she lied. She was entirely too interested. "Sorry," she softened it, hating the lost look in his eyes.

Before she could change her mind, she turned on her heel and left.

CHAPTER 6

"Mr. France was disqualified because he was a dragon," Bastian said with a snarl. "Everyone knows it. Specism is a thing and mythical creatures get the short end of every stick."

"I don't know," Travis said thoughtfully. "They said it was drugs. Besides, Mr. Ireland is a pegasus."

"Maybe they just have something against dragons, then, and not sissy flying horses. And what drugs could possibly survive a dragon's bloodstream?"

"It was some designer thing, specific to dragons," Travis explained, reading from his tablet. They call it gold-shot, and it has some kind of *enhancing* properties."

"Enhancing what?" Breck asked suggestively from across the room.

"Hey, there's Graham!"

The surly landscaper made a brief appearance in the background of the interview on the screen, scowling and vanishing as soon as he realized he was in the field of the camera's view.

In person, Graham grunted and took a drink from his beer.

The Mr. Shifter competition was on the staff television, streaming through the Internet, rather than broadcast television. Shifters weren't acknowledged in all of the countries represented, which made the competition more complicated, and the contest was being hosted through a webpage. At least part of the contestant elimination was done through Internet voting, though there were also a half dozen celebrity judges wandering the resort acting important.

Tex sat at the other end of the couch from Graham, nursing a beer and paying the barest of attention to the screen he was staring through.

"Damn, this place looks great on camera," Travis said proudly. There were aerial shots of the pool, zooming in through the palm trees to the Greek columns and grand steps, flanked on each side by waterfalls. Mr. India was stepping out of the water, and the camera lingered on the water slipping off his dusky skin and the tight, shiny spandex of the very spare swimsuit he was wearing. It was a bit of a disconnect, seeing the sunlit resort when the darkness outside was so complete.

"Man, that French villa is wishing they hadn't screwed up their contract," Breck agreed. Every shot made the resort look good, with gleaming cottages and landscape that was dripping in riotous flowers. There had been multiple shots of the pristine beach, with its jeweled jungle backdrop and crystal blue water. It was the kind of advertising you couldn't buy with money.

"That probably had something to do with Mr. France's disqualification, too," Bastian muttered acidly.

"It could have just been that Mr. France couldn't fake

his way through the part of the contest where he had to actually speak in complete sentences," Travis suggested.

"Not that he has to for the swimsuit portion," Breck countered merrily.

Bastian's face went dark and he rose up out his seat with a growl, but he only pivoted on his foot and left in a grouchy huff.

"What's his problem?" Tex asked, momentarily distracted from his own problems.

Breck shrugged.

Surprisingly, it was Graham who answered. "He had to move his hoard. It's a dragon thing."

"Oh," Breck, Tex, and Travis said in understanding unison.

Bastian had been in a vicious mood since they'd moved out of the hotel, though any of the other staff would have cheerfully said that the house by the cliffs was actually a step up. It wasn't as private, but the rooms were bigger, and the common areas were stunning. The only real problems were that the toilet clogged if you flushed anything larger than a grape, and that Breck refused to tie his bathrobe closed when he was wandering around early in the morning drinking coffee.

The pageant stream went to a sponsored commercial for energy drinks and Travis muted it.

"I have a question," Tex finally started, and stalled out. He had his guitar in his lap, but his fingers were uncharacteristically still on the strings.

"Out with it, Cowboy," Breck prodded him.

"Do you… believe in mates?"

"Hard to deny them," Travis said solemnly.

Graham just grunted, but Tex thought it sounded affirmative.

"I just hope it never happens to me," Breck said, clutching his neck in a choking motion.

"But if it does," Tex pursued. "If it does, it's supposed to be at first sight, right? You're supposed to know immediately."

Even Graham nodded at that.

Travis said, "My grandfather used to say that if you aren't sure, it's just lust."

"It's not just lust," Tex said before he could stop himself.

The others stared at him.

"Cheers!" said Breck. "Who's the lucky girl?"

"You lucky dog," Travis added. "The sex is supposed to be amazing."

Graham gave him a crooked smile and raised his beer can in a toast.

Tex groaned and put his face in his hand, tipping back his hat.

"I just—I don't understand. We met before and it was nothing like this. Not even a spark. And now, she acts like... like..." Tex flailed. "Like she doesn't feel what I do."

"You already met once?" Travis asked, puzzled.

"Years ago, in Austin. Had a little after-hours chat when I was closing a bar I worked at."

"Just a chat, eh?" Breck could make anything sound suggestive.

"Just a chat," Tex said firmly. "She needed a little help and, even though she was gorgeous and willing, nothing actually happened."

"And this time...?" Travis prompted.

Tex pulled his hat back down over his eyes. "Sweet daisies help me. I cannot get her out of my mind. I want to do unspeakable things to her, and I want to get down on my knee and propose on the spot, and she's looking at me like I'm a sun-touched fool."

"Is she a shifter?" Breck asked.

"No," Tex said, just as his bear inside him said, *Yes*.

"*What?*" Tex said in confusion.

"Well, if she's not a shifter, she might not know about mates. Probably, she isn't sure why she's all hot and bothered for *you* in a crowd full of Mr. Shifter contestants." Breck's explanation was plausible.

"Doesn't explain why he didn't get the lightning bolt the first time they met," Travis added thoughtfully.

"Not you," Tex said impatiently. "My bear says she's a shifter. But *she* said she wasn't."

That earned him curious looks.

"Bizarre," Travis said with a shrug.

Graham looked darkly suspicious.

"Have you always been able to tell who's a shifter?" Breck asked curiously.

"Sometimes I can smell it on them, but not always," Tex said, baffled. He poked at his bear curiously, but his companion was distracted, all attention focused on their distant mate. All he could get was— "A wolf. She's a wolf shifter."

"Can you tell what Scarlet is?" Travis asked avidly. Most of the staff had bets going on the topic.

Tex shook his head, shrugging.

Graham shushed them, pointing at the screen, and Travis turned the volume up as the program returned with the interview and videography of Mr. Austria, an eagle shifter with Alps for muscles and a thick Germanic accent.

He was just explaining his plan for implementing world peace when there was a timid tap on the door.

Breck rose to answer it.

"*Excusez-moi!*" came a familiar voice. "I wondered if

Tex was free to, how do you say, walk with me? If he is still up, I know it is late."

"Is that her?" hissed Travis.

Graham gave a lopsided grin and raised an eyebrow at him.

Tex grimaced and shook his head, but rose to his feet and came to the door to see Marie, elbowing Breck out of the way.

"Ma'am," he said politely, touching the rim of his hat. When she stepped back away from the door, he felt obligated to come out into the tropical darkness with her—there was no way he was inviting a lady into the bachelor house to the attention of his housemates. He closed the door behind him, knowing it wouldn't do much good because the house had no air conditioning and all the windows were open. "Let's step up to the staff garden."

She took his arm gladly and Tex tried not to sigh too loudly.

"You have been so kind to me," Marie said, laying her head against his arm. "I just wanted to find some way to thank you."

"Marie," he started, once he thought they were out of easy earshot. There was a bench under a flowering magnolia tree and he sat with her there while he tried to find a way to let her down easy. A single garden lamp barely lit the little garden.

Without warning, Marie launched herself at him, her mouth landing on his demandingly.

Tex didn't want to hurt her and awkwardly tried to pry her off without manhandling her, finally standing up to escape her ardent kisses and insistent hands.

"*Qu'est-ce qui ne va pas?*" she asked breathlessly. "What's wrong? Have I offended you? Am I... not attractive?"

She was wearing something frilly and very low cut;

somehow it had slipped off one shoulder as Tex struggled to get away. As she spoke, her breasts heaved in a way that would have been very distracting indeed if Tex couldn't help but compare them to the shape that Jenny's must be.

Tex had to laugh a little. "Marie, ma'am, you are lovely, and any man would be lucky to win you."

Her eyes were dark and glittered with tears in the faint light. "But you do not find me worthy."

"It's not about worthy," Tex promised sincerely. "If things were different… but there's…"

"Someone else," Marie's voice had an iron edge. "There is another *amour*."

Tex thought about Jenny's haughty dismissal of him and sighed. "It's complicated," he said.

Marie drew her shirt up over her shoulder and sat back, offended dignity in every line of her posture. "If it were not for her?" she pouted.

Tex was already thinking about Jenny again, the flash of spirit in her brown eyes, the curve of her perfect mouth. "If it weren't for her," he agreed plaintively. If it weren't for her, he could sleep at night, could close his eyes without picturing her. He shifted on the bench, embarrassed to find that he was having a physical reaction to just imagining her.

He didn't want Marie to think he was reacting to her, so he focused on where he was again. "Marie, let me walk you back to your room. You're at the next staff house up, right?"

Marie graciously let him escort her, keeping her hand on his arm, but not leaning on him this time.

"Thank you," she said thickly, when they arrived at her door. Tex could hear the sound of the Mr. Shifter contest blaring from the screen in their house, female voices laughing and appraising the contenders. "You are a true gentleman."

Tex tipped his hat at her. "Just trying not to shame the mother who taught me manners," he promised with a little laugh to lighten the mood. "Have a good night, ma'am."

"Oh, I will," Marie answered. Tex couldn't identify the tone of her voice, but was happy that she went inside without further protest.

He walked back down the manicured path to his staff house, decided he was done watching the contest for now, and slipped quietly to his own room.

He shucked off his staff shirt and lay down, to slide at once into dreams about Jenny.

CHAPTER 7

"*I* am very well-known in most of Europe," the photographer told Laura. "Practically a household name. Everyone knows who Juan Lopez is."

Laura made an uninterested noise that was taken as an interested noise by the gold Speedo-clad man wearing so much suntan lotion he looked as greasy as he sounded.

"I would love to photograph you," he said, slipping his sunglasses down to give her a look that was only barely not a leer. "You have this *joyous life* to you. I wish to capture it on film."

Laura knew a line when she heard it. She hooked a finger on her own sunglasses and looked at him over the top in a deliberate mirror of his own. "Nude, of course," she said dryly.

Her sarcasm was lost on him. "Of course. It is the only way to do you justice!"

Laura settled back into her sunchair, realizing that subtlety was not her friend here. "Nope."

"You won't get another opportunity like this! I am an artist..."

"Go find some other naive woman with low self-esteem to try this on," Laura suggested. "I'm not interested, I won't be interested, and I'm not above reporting you to the staff if you continue to harass me."

She tipped her head back and closed her eyes, every other sense alert. "Get lost." She curled her fingers around her water bottle and prepared to throw it at him if the matter escalated.

The photographer sputtered in surprised outrage, then muttered an insult and took himself somewhere else.

"Don't mind if I am," Laura muttered after him, then took a sip of her water. The old her would have fallen for his flattery. He wasn't bad looking, if perhaps a bit outclassed at a tropical resort filled with male pageant contestants and staffed with men who could have given them a run for their money.

But she knew better. He'd picked her because she was wearing a modest one-piece by the pool and wasn't model thin like so many of the beauty coaches and personal assistants. She was probably obvious about dodging Fred at this point, so she looked like easy pickings for the self-esteem pickup… he'd flatter her, she'd decide to do the pictures to make herself feel better about her looks, there would be drinks, a pass that she wouldn't feel good about saying no to. Men suck, she reminded herself. She was done with them.

Except that she couldn't get Tex's face out of her mind. That gorgeous, stunned smile, those clever-looking fingers. The perfect laugh crinkles around his big brown eyes.

No, she thought fiercely. *Done with men.*

Tex was behind the bar, handling the light traffic of the sweltering afternoon. Laura couldn't see him from the pool deck, but she knew he was there. It was hard to pretend that she wasn't irresistibly drawn to him, but he'd been impeccably professional when she had returned to the bar the evening before. He'd clearly been confused by her and Laura hated the longing hurt in his eyes, but chivalry seemed to be his first order of business. He'd filled her drink order without grilling her or pressing her further, keeping conversation to the business at hand.

That was how it was going to be, then. She would pretend there was nothing there, and he would respect the distance she was insisting on.

Laura was wryly aware that this plan would not have worked with anyone less than a perfect cowboy like Tex.

"Can I get you anything, Mademoiselle?"

Laura sat up to find that a young dark-haired woman in a crisp white housekeeping uniform had a tray full of bottled water, one of them open.

"Thank you, no," Laura said, settling back on the lounge. She indicated the half-full bottle she had contemplated throwing at the photographer.

To her surprise, the woman didn't move on right away. "You are enjoying your stay at Shifting Sands, I hope?" she asked leadingly.

Laura considered. If she hadn't been stressing so hard about maintaining her cover, this would have been a perfect vacation spot. The bar was well-stocked, the hotel was comfortable and well-appointed. She loved the aesthetic of the whole place, with its shining tile and riotous jungle gardens. The restaurant could get crowded between the Mr. Shifter events, but Laura recognized that this was a temporary state of affairs and had learned to schedule her visits to the services during times when most of the guests would be busy with the pageant games. If Jenny had been with her, she might have wanted to spend more time watching them like so many of the other visitors, but without her, if felt empty and disappointing.

That, and she kept comparing the contestants to Tex.

It was all too complicated to explain to the maid, so Laura simply said, "I'm having a great time." It wouldn't have been a lie if she hadn't been working so hard to hide her true identity.

"And you know Tex, I think?"

Laura was trying so hard to figure out what kind of accent the maid had—it didn't sound Spanish, she thought —that she wasn't expecting Tex's name, and she started. "I... er... we met once a few years ago. In Austin." It was mostly the truth.

"I see." The woman's icy tone surprised Laura, but as quickly as she recognized it, it was swept away in a bubbling laugh. "He is a great bartender! We love his juggling!"

Taken aback by the pendulum swing of the woman's demeanor, Laura laughed hesitantly along. "Yeah, he's great at it."

"He plays and sings so beautifully, as well, you have heard him?"

Laura shook her head.

"Always with the saddest songs. You are sure you do not want a fresh *eau?*"

"Ew?" Laura said, then her brain caught up with her ear. "Oh, *eau*, water, no, no thank you." A French accent, then.

"Another time," the housekeeper suggested firmly, and her shoes clicked across the tiles firmly. Laura thought it was odd that she didn't pause to offer one of the other sunbathers any water, but perhaps Laura simply hadn't heard her talking to them earlier.

The poolside sun brought her no comfort after that and after a few more moments trying to get comfortable in the chair, Laura abandoned her magazine and decided to return to her room.

Jenny's laptop was sitting on the desk, and Laura sighed and opened it, emotions in a jumble. She was desperate for some kind of closure, some closeness with her lost sister. She probably had some of their email exchanges, neatly filed. Maybe reading over them would make her feel better.

Jenny's wallpaper was a serene tropical scene with a white beach, which made Laura smile crookedly. If only she could see the view out Laura's own window now.

Before she could open the email program, Laura was stopped by a shortcut on the desktop labeled finances—will and life insurance. Of course Jenny would be so organized. When Jenny was halfway through law school, she'd insisted that Laura file a will. Laura had left everything to Jenny, and Jenny had done the same in return. Was there a life insurance policy that named her? But no, they thought it was Laura that was dead, and she'd never taken out a life insurance policy, and she didn't have any money to inherit.

Did Jenny have a policy that named *her*? Jenny was always looking out for her.

Laura wiped away a tear and clicked on the shortcut. It opened a folder with more links—Jenny's bank, copies of legal-looking documents...

A tap on the door startled her, and Laura had to take a deep breath and remind herself that it wasn't like she was *stealing* Jenny's money.

She ignored the person at the door, hoping they would go away, until there was a scratching at the lock that made her realize it was probably housekeeping.

"Oh, thank you, no," she said hastily, getting to her feet. "You can come back later. Or not at all. I can make my own bed, really."

She went to the door, not sure if they'd heard her, and pulled it open to find Fred putting something in his pocket.

"I was worried," he said. "You've been so distant, and have so much to deal with. I wanted to make sure you were alright." He stepped towards her and Laura instinctively moved back, inadvertently inviting him into the room.

Laura smothered a sigh. Would tears only encourage him to stay and try to comfort her? She settled for trying to feign a brave face.

"I'm okay," she promised. "It's hard, and sometimes I just need a break. There are so many people here, you know. It's sometimes a little overwhelming." She gave a trembling smile. "Laura would have loved this place." Too thick?

Fred patted her arm, a strictly paternal and comforting move that still felt awkward. Jenny may have been good friends with him, but Laura hadn't seen him since she moved out on her own nearly ten years ago.

He glanced around, as if he found the moment as awkward as she did, and his eyes fell on Jenny's open laptop. Laura suppressed her urge to leap for it and close the lid.

"There aren't too many people in the restaurant right now," Fred said coaxingly. "There's some kind of photo thing down at the beach, so we could go now and get a good seat for dinner and make an early night of it tonight."

As if sleep would make everything better.

Lacking a good excuse, Laura agreed, closing the laptop as unobtrusively as she could manage before reluctantly following him out.

"Are you enjoying the resort?" Fred asked carefully, as they were served a generous plate of baked fish slathered in a creamy sauce, topped with fresh herbs and served on a bed of fluffy rice.

The restaurant usually only had two gourmet meal selections, but what it lacked in choice, it made up in quality. If she wasn't in the mood for what was available, the buffet always had sandwich ingredients and a few staple dishes to choose from. But Laura had never been less than delighted with what she was served.

"It's lovely here," Laura said, though she knew her tone was lack-luster.

"You're not... sorry you came?" Fred pressed. "I know you haven't been enjoying the pageant events as much as you thought you would."

Laura put on a brave smile. "I'm not sorry I came," she promised.

Fred drew an exaggerated hand over his forehead. "Whew," he clowned. "I would hate to be responsible for convincing you to go on vacation and have it turn out terrible."

Laura felt for him. He was trying so hard to make sure she had a good time, and had been such a good friend of the family. She remembered how he'd been there when their parents had died, making bad jokes to try to cheer them up, and handling all the paperwork and finances that they'd floundered with.

"Have you thought about what you'll do next?" he asked unexpectedly.

Laura froze, and then reminded herself that he was undoubtedly not talking about her plan to disappear in a foreign country.

She toyed with the fog on her water glass and looked down at the suddenly unappetizing fish. "I haven't thought about it," she lied.

"You'll need to have a memorial," Fred told her gently.

"I know neither of you would want a fancy funeral, but you should have something."

Laura took a sip of the ice water to try to loosen the sudden lump in her throat. Jenny deserved a fancy funeral. Probably her lawyer friends would come, all in business black. Her neighbors would turn out, with their neatly-dressed offspring.

Who would come to *her* memorial? Ex-boyfriends? Her grouchy landlady? The guy who delivered her favorite Chinese take-out?

The cartel?

Not for the first time, Laura was certain that the wrong person had been in that car.

"Yeah, you're right," she agreed faintly, knowing she looked sick.

Fred patted her hand. "You leave all the details to me, sweetie. I'll arrange a nice, quiet memorial and can take care of all the paperwork."

It was an echo from years ago, and Laura felt like she was seventeen again, lost and afraid and adrift.

The only difference was that Jenny wasn't here to cling to.

There was a sudden rise in the hum of conversation at the restaurant as guests began to arrive en mass, laughing loudly about the beach-side sunset photoshoot.

Laura choked down the last of her fish and told Fred she planned to head to bed early. "There's a marathon kick-off pretty early tomorrow that I'd like to catch," she said, mostly meaning it.

He gave her a fatherly hug that she couldn't politely dodge and stayed for dessert while she fled.

CHAPTER 8

"*W*hat's next on the Mr. Shifter schedule?" Travis asked, collapsing onto a stool at the end of the bar. "I got the generator for the laundry room back up again, but I have no idea how long it will keep working. Tell Breck that the second washer needs his special kick."

Tex poured him an orange juice. "I see a bed in *your* schedule," he suggested.

"One more stop," Travis protest, downing the orange juice. "Broken fan in cottage three."

"Hasn't that fan been broken twice this week already?" Bastian, just off lifeguard duty as the sun went down, slid onto a recently abandoned stool. Most of the post photo-shoot crowd had milled off for dinner at the restaurant and Tex could hear them on the deck above, laughing and carousing. He'd just sent a tray of fancy drinks up with one of the waitresses who was running her tail off.

"I'm beginning to think they're breaking it on purpose," Travis said darkly.

"Probably, they're just enjoying watching you climb up

on that ladder," Bastian teased. "Everyone's in the Mr. Shifter mood for a little show."

Tex served Bastian a shot of cinnamon whiskey, neat, and consulted the resort schedule. "To answer your first question, Travis, it looks like early tomorrow morning is the Mr. Speed event, the marathon to the airport and back. And tomorrow evening is the Mr. Fur, Fins, or Feather animal event."

"How does that even work?" Bastian asked, tossing down his shot. "I mean, how would you judge between all the different animals? Cage match?"

Travis laughed, pushing his glass back over the counter. "I think they are evaluated against species ideals and assigned values by expert judges. I know Lydia's got her girls booked for the entire afternoon for grooming services. Guests are grumbling about how hard it is to get any spa services."

"I know we should be grateful that business is so good after a long dry spell, but I will be very glad to have things back to some kind of normal," Tex said wearily. He glanced longingly at his guitar, leaning in the corner of the bar. Most days, he had plenty of opportunity to sit behind the bar and play. This week, between the madhouse of guests and assisting Travis in getting the resort into top working order, he hadn't touched the strings. Every spare moment was spent restocking, or cleaning, or repairing.

"Speaking of normal," Bastian said, raising an eyebrow.

Tex looked at him blankly.

"What's up with your mate?" Travis finished for him.

Tex was glad that a guest sidled up and requested a drink, but when they wandered off to the pool deck with it, Travis and Bastian were still staring at him expectantly.

"Aren't you too busy for gossip?" he asked crossly. "I am."

Travis and Bastian exchanged knowing looks.

"She still denying it?" Travis asked pityingly.

"It doesn't make any sense," Tex said, knowing he sounded as whiny as he felt. "I mean I've always felt unlucky in love, but this is ridiculous. How can she not feel this?"

"Why do you always say that?" Travis asked. "That bit about being unlucky in love."

Tex shrugged. "It just always seemed that way. I'd get my courage up to ask a girl out... right after she got asked out by the high school jock. Or that date where my truck broke down on my way to the restaurant and she ended up marrying the waiter."

"Brutal," Bastian agreed. "And now your own mate is pretending there's no bond between you."

Tex let out a breath he didn't know he was holding. "I can't stop thinking about her. I can't get her face—or her body—out of my mind. I don't sleep without dreaming about her."

"Sounds like those songs you love to sing," Travis teased kindly. "The sadder the better, right?"

Tex groaned and pinched the bridge of his nose. "I don't know what to do," he confessed.

"Another round of margaritas!" one of the tables called.

The harried looking waitress scrambled through the back door with a tray of empty glasses. "I need a sidecar, a ginger snap, two blended margaritas and one on the rocks, no salt. Two pilsners, one Guinness, and a Budweiser."

"Who the hell goes to a tropical luxury resort and orders a Budweiser?" Bastian asked, getting up from his stool to let Tex get back to work. "Come on, I'll hold your ladder, Travis, and make sure no one tells you about anything broken before you can get a decent night's sleep. Breck can kick the generator if the laundry room goes black again."

"That's what I'm afraid of," Travis said darkly. "He can handle the machines, but I don't like him doing the electrical stuff. I've seen what that man can do to a fusebox!"

They left Tex to mix drinks and think dark thoughts about things sadder than any country song he'd ever sung.

CHAPTER 9

Sunrise yoga in the recreation center hadn't even started when Laura joined the growing throng at the very top of the resort.

Laura yawned and wished she'd thought to swing by the restaurant for a latte before coming to the start of the marathon. Several smarter guests carried steaming to-go cups.

The view was arguably worth the early morning. To one side was the vista down over the terraced resort, with it's charming cottages and grand architecture. The pool from here was a huge blue jewel, and the ocean beach beyond was a sliver of white caressed by turquoise water. The early morning sun set silver light in the jungle tree-tops, casting dappled shadows everywhere.

The other side was a sea of beefcake. The finalists were all wearing the barest of running shorts, and only one of them had opted for a tanktop... and it was one so tight and scant it was barely worth the effort.

There was more gleaming manflesh, stretching and

warming up in provocative positions, than Laura would expect to find in a magazine for lonely women.

She found her cheeks heating, just watching the spectacle, but she kept thinking about what the bartender, Tex, would look like. She hadn't gotten a glimpse of his ass, but she could imagine that it was much like Mr. Brazil's, given their similar body build. Mr. Brazil obligingly bent over to stretch his hamstrings and gave her an amazing view of his spandex-clung butt and the barely contained package beyond.

The girls next to Laura giggled and fanned themselves.

It suddenly occurred to Laura to wonder if Tex had a pair of assless chaps, to match his other over-the-top cowboy accessories, and then, of course, it occurred to her how much *fun* such a garment might be.

We could find out, Laura's wolf suggested.

We could not, Laura replied sternly.

One of the celebrity hostesses, a little bottle-blonde woman named Jessica Linn, looking more than a little hungover, banged on her clipboard. "Are you rolling?" she asked the cameraman.

"When you're ready," he said.

"I'm ready to get this over with," she snapped. "Why would they schedule this so early?"

"Gets too hot later," Mr. Canada guessed over his sunglasses. He looked as dragged out as Jessica did.

Mr. Ireland, by contrast, was bouncing in place, obviously eager to go.

"Alright," Jessica said. "Listen up, studs. We're going to go over the rules before we turn on the cameras and I don't want to have to say things more than twice." She pointed down the road behind them. "You'll be running down that road to the airport, and back up. It's about two miles each direction, lots of winding, lots of hills, mostly under jungle cover. We've got cameramen in several key spots, and the video camera will be in a Jeep behind you for part of the way. There's also a drone that will be following you. There is no shifting allowed, this is human legs only."

Laura wasn't surprised—it wouldn't be much of a race between a pegasus and a peacock, but Mr. India looked lean and fit; she thought he might give Mr. Ireland some competition.

"The winner will be awarded the Mr. Speed trophy in the final awards ceremony, and there's a ribbon or something for the second place. I don't know, who cares." Jessica fanned herself with her clipboard. "I'm bound by the insurance company to let you know that you are not covered for egregious injury due to special shifter riders, blah blah, don't be a dumbass and step in a gopher hole. We're not medi-vaccing you. Do they even have gophers here? Oh, let's just get this started. I need some cheers, ladies."

She fluffed her hair and pinched her cheeks, pasting on the most plastic smile that Laura had ever seen and gestured at the cameraman in the back of the poised Jeep.

"Welcome back to the World Mr. Shifter events!" she squealed. The girls gathered around Laura gave ear-splitting shrieks and applause, and the Mr. Shifter competitors stepped up their stretching and posing as the camera panned around.

Laura clapped half-heartedly.

"Oh, it's such a shame Mr. Ireland is married," one of the audience members near Laura lamented.

"I thought that being single was one of the criteria!" another protested.

"No, that's the *International* Mr. Shifter competition, this is the *World* Mr. Shifter. These guys don't even require that you have modeling experience. Mr. Ireland doesn't."

"What does he do?" The first woman was practically drooling.

"Firefighter, I heard."

"Oh, he can put out my fires any day."

"Show us your best cheeks, gentlemen!" Jessica was saying enthusiastically.

The Mr. Shifters lined up at the white chalk line that had been drawn on the road, pausing to flex and preen and dust invisible things off their shoulders.

This would have been a lot more fun with Jenny to snark with, Laura couldn't help thinking. Or if she could stop imagining Tex as a contestant. He looked like he could make a steep, four mile jog without getting winded.

Probably carrying a tray of drinks.

In assless chaps.

Laura shook her head firmly, and turned around to walk back down into the resort before they finished the introductions and the starting gun was fired. Maybe this way she could beat the rush on the restaurant and get a good seat and a peaceful latte.

CHAPTER 10

*T*he restaurant was one level above the bar, with an expanse of open indoor seating and a spacious deck that looked down over the bar deck, the pool deck below, and the beach beyond that. Tex found that looking down over the uppermost deck gave an interesting perspective to the view that he usually enjoyed as he worked.

Tex closed the bar about midnight and wasn't often up this early, but when the sun rose at five and the birds came alive with the light, he gave up the pretense of trying to sleep and came to rustle breakfast from the kitchens. Chef, raising an eyebrow at him, didn't question his early appearance or the circles under his eyes. He just gave him a plate with a fresh bun stuffed with an arcane egg and sausage scramble.

Marie had been helping in the kitchen and gave him a long, plaintive look, but she didn't attempt to stop him when he left.

Scarlet allowed the staff to eat anything they wanted

from the kitchens or the buffet, but discouraged them from mingling with the guests to eat their food. Tex had every intention of heading back to the conference room with his culinary prize, or even retreating to the closed bar to eat it there.

But then he felt her. *Jenny*, he thought and everything was wrong about the way her name sounded in his head.

He hadn't caught more than a glimpse of her the day before, desperately busy during the morning helping Travis piece together some questionable plumbing at one of the smaller cottages, and even busier at the bar after dinner until midnight. Celebrities, he found, came with more ridiculous demands for their drinks than any clientele he'd ever served. Never had so many olives been found unsatisfactory or mixing methods been called into question.

He'd been grateful not to have the time to think about Jenny, because she came with such a pang of pain and confusion.

Now, though, she was here, at the same level he was, being seated at a table that completely blocked a subtle escape. He either had to walk within arms reach behind her or walk out straight in front of her.

Frozen with indecision, Tex only watched her, doing what he suspected was a terrible job of camouflaging himself in the potted plants near the railing.

Even from here, she was so beautiful. Her dark hair was soft over her mahogany shoulders. Tex was mesmerized by the little motions she made with her hand as she ordered and the flicker of a smile over her mouth at some joke of Breck's.

He was shallowly glad when she responded coolly to the head waiter's obvious flirtation and irrationally angry when Breck was able to make her laugh with his pout.

Tex took another bite of Chef's breakfast concoction and finally made the decision to try to creep behind Jenny. It was possible she wouldn't notice him on that route, even if it would take more willpower to be that close to her and keep going.

Then he paused, trying to figure out what felt so wrong.

The sounds of the restaurant were all exactly right: the low murmur of conversation with the occasional laugh, and the clink of cutlery and the sounds of eating. More guests were arriving as the morning grew later, and there were the sounds of chairs scooting as they took their seats. It was busier than it usually was, but that had become the new normal with the booming event business.

Nothing looked out of the ordinary; servers bringing plates of food and specialty coffee drinks, clearing off tables and refilling coffee and water. The guests varied between bleary-eyed and clearly fighting hangovers, to energetic looking, probably fresh from Lydia's morning yoga. The early light shimmered over the open deck in ripples through the potted plant leaves.

There was nothing out of the ordinary about the little breeze that blew in over the open dining area, or the birds that sang.

It was the smell.

It wasn't just the food, and the breakfast drinks, and the tang of the jungle plants. He could also smell each person, under whatever cologne or deodorant they were wearing, and whatever they had brushed their teeth with. It was a tangled, many-faceted sense, and part of it was... wrong.

Bear was roaring in his head as Tex dropped his breakfast, shifting as he leaped across the room.

In one swift swipe of an enormous paw, the latte that

was being served to Jenny went flying, to shatter against one of the support columns.

After an understandable flurry of gasps and shrieks, the chairs that Tex had knocked over stilled, and the dining room went silent. Tex was aware that he was the focus of absolutely everyone, forks frozen over plates, some of the guests even standing in alarm. Jenny's latte dripped slowly to the floor in a foamy mess.

He opened his mouth to explain, but it came out in a rumbling growl.

"What is the meaning of this?"

Tex heard the distinctive click of Scarlet's shoes before he saw her, pacing decisively towards them.

"I had to save her," Tex tried to say, but it was an ursine whine.

"Would you care to explain this, Mr. Williams? I suspect your human shape would be more useful to communication." Scarlet crossed her arms and waited.

Tex sheepishly shifted, realizing that he was completely naked and that his staff uniform had been completely destroyed in his rush. He was keenly aware of Jenny, plastered back in her chair in shock, and to some lesser degree, aware of Breck, who was still holding an empty hand out to her, frozen in place. He glanced behind him to realize that he'd broken one table leaping over it, and cracked several chairs. His hat was tottering on the edge of the railing, next to a broken planter littered with shreds of his polo shirt. Graham was going to have words with him about that.

He cleared his throat. "I apologize for the disruption, ma'am," he said to Scarlet, with a nod to Jenny. "I... ah, smelled something."

One of Scarlet's eyebrows inched towards her neat hairline. "You smelled something."

"Yes ma'am," Tex said firmly, drawing himself up to his full height despite his urge to grab a napkin from the table to cover himself with. "A bear's nose is more powerful than a bloodhound's, and I smelled something." He pointed at the coffee drink that had puddled on the floor. "That's poisoned."

The gasp from the audience was theatrically perfect.

Scarlet's second eyebrow joined the first. "Poisoned?"

There was the snap of a cellphone camera shutter, and Scarlet's head pivoted to glare at the photographer. The woman gave a quavering smile against her glower and put her phone sheepishly down on the table at once.

That released a titter of quiet conversation and speculation and Breck sat down heavily in the empty chair opposite Jenny.

"Damn, Tex. Give a little warning next time you're going to be a two-thousand pound brown bear and slap a mug out of my hand," the waiter said breathlessly.

"It's Jenny, right?" Scarlet said to the wide-eyed woman.

At her silent nod, Scarlet extended a hand. "I apologize for the disruption of your meal, but if I could ask you a few questions more privately?"

Jenny stood up, exchanging a brief, terrified look with Tex.

"Breck, please see that we have a record of everyone— staff and guests—that were in and out of here this morning." Scarlet's voice was deceptively calm. "Collect as much of the coffee as you can, and keep the pieces of the mug. Get the rest of this cleaned up and make sure that our guests enjoy their breakfast."

Breck came to his feet smartly, and immediately started getting his dazed staff in order as people slowly (and suspiciously) returned to their meals.

Tex trailed after Scarlet and Jenny protectively, shaken by the stark fear in her eyes. He didn't know what she was so desperately afraid of, but he knew that he had to protect her.

CHAPTER 11

The bear should have frightened her. A gigantic, snarling brown bear had loped across the deck at her, destroying tables and chairs, and smashed the coffee cup from her very fingertips. Laura knew that she should have been quaking in her shoes at the near-assault, and she wasn't sure why she hadn't feared for her life at any point in that blurry moment.

It was Tex's words that shot cold terror into her heart.

Poison.

Her latte had been *poisoned*.

That meant the cartel had found her. She'd been followed under her sister's name to this foreign resort and they were still trying to get to her.

There was no place in the world that was safe for her.

"What kind of poison was it?" Scarlet asked, once they were out of the restaurant and in a little office off the kitchens with the door closed. Laura sank into the only available chair without asking, sure that her shaking knees weren't going to hold her any longer.

Tex took an apron off a hook near the door and used it to do a poor job of covering his nakedness. Laura was grateful for that much coverage; a completely naked Tex was extremely distracting. She kept imagining what she would do to him, what his skin would feel like if she touched him.

"Rattlesnake venom," Tex said confidently.

Scarlet frowned at him. "We don't have any rattlesnake shifters registered among the staff or the guests. Are you sure?"

"I'm sure, ma'am," he said firmly. "We found a rattlesnake nest on the ranch when I was a kid, and I will never forget that scent."

Scarlet turned her sharp emerald eyes to Laura, and Laura shivered at the intensity in them. Surely this woman was looking right through her flimsy disguise.

"Do you know why someone would attempt to poison you?"

"No," Laura lied, hoping her squeak sounded sincere. She could think of at least two reasons—either the cartel she'd been reluctantly working for thought she'd snitched, or the rival cartel had figured out who she was. Either one of them would want her out of the picture, and had already tried to do that, taking her sister instead. She swallowed the grief that welled up in her throat.

"Would rattlesnake poison have killed you?" Scarlet's gaze was direct and unnerving.

It would have killed Jenny, Laura realized with a start. Her sister wasn't a shifter. Laura might have burned off the poison if she'd shifted, but Jenny definitely wouldn't have been able to. She felt safe giving an uncertain shrug, not really sure who she was answering for.

"You represented Mr. Stubbins, the producer of the

Mr. Shifter event, when he broke contract with the previous resort, didn't you?" Scarlet suggested. "Could there be some hard feelings there?"

Laura had only the foggiest idea what Jenny had done with the contract, or how she had handled that case; most of what she knew about law was based on sensational cop shows. "I suppose there could be?" she said hesitantly, hoping it wouldn't raise questions about the details.

"Wouldn't that mean Mr. Stubbins was a target?" Tex suggested. Laura could have kissed him. Not that she didn't already want to kiss him, with his gorgeous, suntanned muscles not at all covered by the tiny apron he was wearing.

Scarlet pursed her lips thoughtfully and said decisively, "I'm going to have some trusted extra security assigned to him. Tell Graham to clean up and report to the office. Travis has got too much to do." She looked at Tex appraisingly. "You keep an eye on Ms. Smith." Tex thought there was a hint of a smile in the corner of her mouth. "I'll report this to the authorities, of course, but they're not likely to react quickly."

Authorities were the last thing that Jenny wanted to involve, but she couldn't very well say that. Everything was unraveling far too rapidly for her to follow.

"I'm very sorry that you've run into this trouble at our resort," Scarlet said sincerely. "We will do our very best to find the person responsible and keep you protected in the meantime."

Was Scarlet afraid of a lawsuit? Laura abruptly remembered that she was supposedly a lawyer and it was probably a valid concern. "I'm sure it's not your fault," she said faintly. Probably that wasn't very lawyer-y of her to say.

Scarlet gave her an unexpected smile. "I'm sure it's not," she agreed dryly. Then, to Laura's dismay, she added, "I would love to consult with you at some time regarding the Shifting Sands contract. I've been butting heads with the owner's lawyer about some of our lease details, and I would appreciate an experienced set of eyes on the wording."

It was everything Laura could do not to squirm and start crying. One wrong word out of her mouth would betray her masquerade now. She kept her gaze locked with Scarlet with effort, but she knew that her hands would be shaking if they weren't clenched tightly in her lap.

"I would pay for your time, of course," Scarlet added, guessing the cause of her discomfort incorrectly. "Now, I've got paperwork to file and samples to store. I'll be taking witness statements from the guest and staff most of the day. If you need anything, be sure to let me know."

Then she was sweeping out, pulling out her cellphone as she went, and the silence in her wake was awkward and deep as Laura kept dragging her eyes away from Tex.

Who was still wearing nothing but an apron.

"I'm so sorry I frightened you," he said, in that thick southern drawl.

Laura gave a strangled sound that was meant to be a laugh. "Frighten me?" she chuckled. "You saved my life." She found that tears were gathering in her eyes against her will. All of her resolve seemed to have vanished in Scarlet's wake.

Tex looked horrified. "Oh, ma'am, no!" He knelt before her, taking her unresisting hands in his own big ones.

"Don't call me ma'am," Laura sniffed.

"Jenny…"

"I'm not Jenny." The words were out before she could stop them.

Tex blinked at her, but kept looking at her with those painfully trusting eyes. "I thought…?"

"Laura. I'm Jenny's twin sister, Laura. Laurelangelina Lily."

"You're… not… Jenny."

Were they back to 'he's an idiot?'

It was just a shame he was such a *gorgeous* idiot.

"Why would you do that for me?" she asked before she thought about it. "Save me, I mean."

"I love you," Tex replied.

Laura's breath caught in her throat. "What?!" It was absurd. Mating wasn't *love*. It wasn't *love* that was making her nethers heat up. It wasn't *love* that made her think about the way Tex's hands would feel on her skin.

But somehow, hearing him say the words was a knife-twist to the gut in a new and agonizing way.

It felt like hope.

Flustered, Tex twisted the apron in his big hands, which made it cover even less of him. Laura caught a tantalizing glimpse of his half-hard member before he shifted uncomfortably.

"I don't mean I *love* you, exactly. I hardly know you. And apparently I know you less than I thought, since the you I knew wasn't you. But I… I couldn't let you get poisoned. Not that I'd let anyone get poisoned, but you… you're *everything*."

It sounded like a line. In his ridiculous cowboy accent, it sounded like it had been written for the most awful movie in the world.

And Laura believed every syllable of it.

She believed that she was everything to him, that, however deluded he might be, he believed she hung the stars. No matter what happened, how stupid she was, he would come galloping for her over any obstacle. He was her knight in a cowboy hat. He was her... *everything*.

Without meaning to, Laura reached out to touch his face.

He was looking up at her adoringly, and when her fingertips brushed his jaw, he caught her hand in his own and kissed it.

Was there no end to his dramatic gallantry? His mouth on her knuckles was more potent than the liquor he'd served her, and Laura was grateful she was sitting; her knees were suddenly very shaky, and she was uncomfortably aware of all her intimate parts.

When she didn't make any motion to withdraw her hand, he turned it over and kissed the inside of her wrist, a place that Laura would never have guessed was so sensitive. Every nerve in her body was on fire, desperate for more of this man's gentle touches.

He wasn't half-hard any longer. The apron was a tent across his lap and Laura was mesmerized by the promise of it.

She swallowed hard. "I'm not in a good place right now," she said, her voice husky. "There's a reason I was pretending to be my own sister."

Tex looked up at her trustingly, not relinquishing her hand. "I'm sure it's a great reason," he said, and there was a catch to his breath that told Laura he was as affected by her presence as she was by his.

"Don't you care what it is?" Laura wondered if she should feel insulted by his lack of concern. But she'd had plenty of experience with jerks who only wanted sex and this didn't feel anything like that.

Tex kissed the inside of her forearm, the stubble of his jaw tickling her skin. Then he looked up at her and said sincerely, "I will protect you from anything. Whoever you fear, I will fight. Whenever you flee, I will find you. Whatever you choose to tell me, that will be enough."

Laura had no defense equal to those words, and fell forward to press her mouth to his.

CHAPTER 12

*T*he apron had been flimsy protection, but when Laura flowed into his lap, the cloth was suddenly an imposition.

She was more intoxicating than the finest whiskey, her mouth was sweeter than chocolate. Tex, slid his hands up her shoulders to cup her jaw so he could kiss her more deeply.

His words had barely scraped the surface of his feelings. He craved her, wanted to be buried inside of her, but more than that, he wanted to protect her, to worship her. She felt like forever.

Then her hand reached beneath the apron, giving him just the barest touch, and he had to gasp for breath.

"You can't go back out there like this," Laura teased him, her voice quiet near his ear.

"The resort *is* clothing optional," Tex wheezed, trying to match her light-hearted tone and failing.

"Clothing is one thing," Laura said chidingly. "This would be just obscene."

"Not... sure... what... to-" Tex couldn't even come up

with a coherent sentence, not with her nails sliding tantalizingly over him.

She leaned in and kissed him again, and this time, Tex had no doubt how she intended to make him presentable again. He stroked the silky skin of her neck, keeping his fingers from clawing her with effort, and tugged the straps of her tank top and bra down to expose a soft shoulder to kiss.

"Besides," she said, in a rich, husky voice as she pulled back, "I don't want to share this view with anyone."

Tex had to bite back a whimper—one of her hands was teasing his hard cock, and the other was pulling the apron off over his head.

"You have an advantage over me," he said as he kissed her. "Let me... oh..."

Her fingers circled his member distractingly and when she pulled her hand away, he groaned at the loss, only to be delighted when she used it to help shuck off her tank top and unclasp her bra in one smooth motion.

Tex froze, mesmerized by the swell of her breasts, and the beauty of her exposed belly. Her nipples hardened in the chill of the office and Tex reached to rub his thumbs over each of them.

Laura gave a noise of pleasure and Tex pulled her closer with a hand cupping each breast, to kiss her jaw, her earlobe, her neck, and then feast on a collarbone before letting himself kiss his way down to the luscious breasts.

He couldn't pause there long, too wound with need and it didn't take much to wrestle her shorts and lacy underwear from her curvy hips. He lay her down on the clear desk and kissed his way down her stomach to pause for a moment at the lightly furred mound above her treasure. A careful breath made Laura cry out wordlessly, and a soft kiss made her arch up to him in need.

"Fuck me," she said, when he might have paused or tried to take a softer path. "Just fuck me, Cowboy."

Tex was eager to oblige.

He slid her to the edge of the desk and lifted her willing leg. If he'd been any harder, he felt he could have burst on the spot and when he pressed himself at her waiting entrance, she was already slick with her own juices.

Entering her was like perfect music; a slow crescendo of pleasure from a plateau of anticipation and need that already felt like a new high. He had to bite his lip not to simply thrust at her like an animal in rut. She deserved a crafted love-making, a worship of luxurious intimacy. Bad enough that he was sneaking with her in Chef's office instead of laying her down on silk sheets in a shower of flower petals, he wasn't going to make a schoolboy's hash of their first coupling.

His bear had other thoughts.

She is ours, he growled inside Tex's head. *Ours to take and love and protect. Our mate. Our all.*

Tex had to find the melody of a slow song in his head to keep his rhythm from becoming frantic. At every sweet thrust, Laura rose to him with a moan of delight and desire. Her hands at his arms left scratches of need and when she writhed in the grip of an orgasm that drove a blissful cry from her perfect lips, Tex lost any sense of slowness and simply fell into his own frantic release.

CHAPTER 13

$\mathcal{L}$ aura was used to sex as an escape from her crappy life. She enjoyed the way problems dissolved for a short time in the hot wake of passion.

But it had never been like this. She didn't feel like she was using Tex for a few moments of ignoring reality and she didn't for an instant feel like he was using her.

He loved her, however he stumbled over the semantics of it.

His touch wasn't just about his pleasure, or even about her pleasure, or their pleasure. It was a bone-deep need, a connection at a level beyond skin. She felt like she'd been placed on an altar and worshiped, not taken in a tiny, barren office on a chilly metal desk as a matter of convenience.

Even after they were done, breath ragged and heart-beats loud in the little room, he didn't let go of her, pulling him up so they were both standing. His strong arms held her up, and he continued stroking her back and shoulders as the moment passed.

"I will never call myself unlucky in love again," he declared, to Laura's amusement.

"You might reconsider that when you realize what you've gotten into," she told him, finally drawing away.

She recovered her tank top and dressed. Tex gave the apron a wry smile and put it back on, then settled back to watch her getting dressed.

"Enjoying the show?" she needled him, shimmying back into her shorts. She gave him an extra, unnecessary jiggle.

"It's almost as much fun as watching you take them off," Tex promised.

Once they were basically presentable, Laura crossed her arms and regarded him thoughtfully.

Tex gazed back, unafraid, and Laura felt like it was a challenge.

"Let me tell you what's going on," she said, settling into the office chair and putting her feet up on the desk.

Tex rather belatedly locked the door and then took a seat opposite, mirroring her posture. He wiggled his bare toes at her.

Laura didn't let herself smile at them.

"I worked for the cartel in south Los Angeles."

Tex took his feet off the desk, but continued to gaze at her as she had hung the moon.

"I didn't mean to," she promised, suddenly not wanting to betray that naive trust. "I have—I've had—terrible taste in men. One of my old boyfriends got me a job, an easy job. They found out I was a shifter, and they had me pretend to be a pet, and I could make... deliveries. I swear, I didn't know who I was really working for, I didn't ask questions about what I was taking places. They paid well, and... I was tired of asking Jenny for money. I thought I was being responsible, finally taking care of myself."

Laura made herself shut her mouth around the continued excuses she wanted to give.

"And your sister?"

Tears unexpectedly welled up in Laura's eyes. Every time that she remembered Jenny, it was like the shock of her loss was all new again.

Tex was around the desk before she could stop him, gathering her into his strong arms. "It's okay, kitten. I'm here. You can tell me."

"She was the best sister," Laura sobbed into his bare shoulder. "She was so smart and kind and *good*. As soon as I found out what I was doing, I tried to get out. I told them I quit, and I went to Jenny and told her everything. But they told me not to tell anyone, and they must have found out, because when she took my car out, it crashed, and she never came back, and they must have *done* something, because she's a good driver, and she wouldn't make a mistake like that."

Tex rocked her in his arms, holding her tight and smoothing her hair back from her face. "It wasn't your fault."

Laura pushed him away, viciously, tears still streaming down her face. "It was entirely my fault," she cried. "They sabotaged my car, and she got caught in the cross-fire. If I hadn't been tangled up in the wrong people, if I hadn't gone to her for help, if I hadn't let her go get things for me…"

Tex looked conflicted, but resolute. "It wasn't your fault," he repeated. "You don't know for sure it wasn't an accident."

Feeling almost hysterical, Laura insisted, "What else would it be? And now they've followed me here, and I'm not safe anywhere…"

Once again, Tex gathered her into his arms, slowly, gently, giving her every opportunity to push him away.

Laura didn't want to push him away. She wanted to snuggle up against those burly arms and beautiful shoulders and let Tex keep everything bad in the world away from her. She wanted to let him be her hero and save her from everything.

Even if she knew he couldn't.

Once she had cried herself out, Tex offered his apron to wipe her cheeks. "Could Fred have tipped them?"

Laura scoffed. "Fred? No. He thinks I'm Jenny, which let me tell you, is getting hard to pull off. I swear, he keeps talking legalese and finance at me and I have to nod and stuff food in my mouth instead of answering. I'm going to gain a hundred pounds if I keep this up."

"You both knew him?"

"He was a friend of our dad's, and worked at the same law business. They were up for partners in the firm at the same time. My dad got the spot, but he and my mom died in a car accident just a few weeks later. Fred was really great to us during that time, helped us get through everything after they died, and set up the loan that got Jenny through school. He even helped Jenny get a job with the firm, after college."

Just as Laura realized she was babbling, there was a knock at the door, and the two scrambled to their feet, looking guilty.

"Why is my door locked?" Chef demanded from the other side.

Laura straightened her tank top one last time and nodded to Tex when he went to open the door.

"Sorry, Chef," he said contritely. "We were just leaving."

Chef, a large, distinguished older man, stood with his

arms crossed, glaring them down. "What have you done in here?" he demanded. Then he pinched the bridge of his nose. "No, I don't want to know. Just get out. And don't ever bring that apron back."

Glancing at each other like erring schoolchildren, barely able to keep the giggles from their lips, Laura and Tex fled, hand-in-hand.

"Don't worry about Chef," Tex told her, giving her a quick kiss at the back door to the restaurant. "He's just grouchy because Magnolia isn't here this week and we rented her cottage to someone else for the event. He doesn't even use this office most of the time."

He escorted her chivalrously to her hotel room, acting nonchalant about his apron-clad bare body, and Laura noticed with amusement that everyone they met took it perfectly in stride.

It was, after all, a clothing-optional shifter's resort, hosting a male beauty pageant.

Nothing seemed too odd for this place.

CHAPTER 14

*O*ne advantage to being a bartender was that Tex got a front-seat to all the best and worst of the guest-watching at Shifting Sands.

He got to watch the producer, Gregory Stubbins, have a shouting show-down with his cameraman, Bam Stagger (Tex guessed it was an assumed name, but never heard him referred to as anything else). Gregory didn't go anywhere without his new black-suited bodyguard since the attempt on Jenny's—Laura's—life, and Tex felt sorry for the stoically sweating rock of a man who shadowed the obnoxious jerk.

Jessica Linn, the tiny blonde celebrity host, got falling down drunk every afternoon at about 2, to sober up in time for whatever evening event she had to announce. She was at best unkind to the resort staff, and at worst, a raging harpy. She thought Tex was a dreamboat, though, so she was slobberingly pleasant to him.

Tex would have rathered she wasn't.

The photographer, Juan Lopez, was constantly taking

candid photographs that Tex strongly suspected would be sold to tabloids later, or used for blackmail, when he wasn't hitting on woman after unsuspecting woman.

Tex's opinion of the Mr. Shifter competitors who frequented the bar ranged from sheer pity, through amusement, into active dislike. Mr. Canada completely failed to uphold his country's reputation for politeness. Mr. India was a class act. Mr. South Africa made Tex very, very wary and raised his bear's hackles. Mr. Brazil was a complete jerkface, flanked by a beauty coach who was at least as bad. Tex thought he might like Mr. United States, even if he was almost a caricature of laziness. Mr. Ireland never took off his glittery green pageant banner and never stopped talking (though his charming wife often stepped in and pointed him in the direction of distractions with a wry smile).

Tex sniffed, literally and figuratively, making even more conversation than he usually did. He got Mr. Ireland talking about his job, firefighting, and then despaired of ever getting him to stop. He got Mr. Austria talking nostalgically about growing up in the Alps, and Mr. India, after a few beers, talked about living in the slums of Delhi. Mr. Japan's beauty assistant was a shy woman that would only take lemon tea, but Tex got her to tell him about climbing Mt Fuji and laughed over her fear of bees.

"They are very large bees," she said, with an embarrassed smile.

Tex commiserated with a story about being chased by angry bees on his farm and convinced her to tell him about Mr. Japan and how she'd gotten involved in the contest.

None of them seemed to have any motive for hurting Jenny. Or Laura, as far as Tex could tell. Most of them only knew who she was because of the incident with the latte.

It was everything Tex could do not to blabber about Laura himself. He wanted to tell everyone about her, to describe her perfect strength and get them to agree that she had the most perfect brown eyes. He caught himself daydreaming about the slow smile she gave him, and the velvet softness of her skin.

But customers, especially the women, didn't want to hear about his perfect mate. They wanted to think his eyes were only for them and as long as Tex was trying to get information out of them, he was willing to indulge them in that delusion.

"Masterfully done," Breck told him, after watching him get Mr. Canada's assistant to tell him all about Mr. Canada's failed hockey career. There was a lull in the traffic at the bar for a moment, while Mr. Ireland demonstrated a fireman's carry at the other end of the deck, to his American wife's laughing dismay. Breck was helping serve drinks while the restaurant was between meals; as busy as things were, none of the staff were enjoying much downtime.

"I'm no closer to finding a motive for poisoning Laura than when I started," Tex said mournfully. "And these people drink like fishes; our stock is never going to last through the closing cere—"

A scream from behind the bar interrupted him.

"This is getting to be a habit," Tex said, grabbing his baseball bat and rounding the bar at a run. Breck followed, grabbing a bottle off the bar as a makeshift weapon.

As girly as the scream had been, it came from Juan Lopez, the photographer.

Graham, teeth bared, was holding Juan's throat in one hand, hedge clippers in the other.

"I didn't mean to," Juan was stuttering, clutching his camera. "It was just, the leaves were in the shot, you know, and they were casting shadows I didn't want, and it was just a plant, and you have to frame the shot just so, and I'm famous in Europe, you know…"

He trailed off to a squeak as Tex handed his bat to Breck and strode forward to lay a careful hand on Graham's arm.

"It's okay Graham, he didn't mean any harm. We can't hurt the guests, come on, let him go." He wasn't foolish enough to say that they were only plants. You never said that to Graham.

With a predatory snarl, Graham abruptly let go of the struggling man, leaving him gasping and staggering.

He gave one angry snap of the hedge clippers that made Juan give a thin little shriek, then turned on his heel and left, white gravel crunching under his feet.

Breck actually laughed and offered Juan the bottle he was holding. "Don't ever cut Graham's plants," he told the gasping Juan. "It's right in the resort contract."

"Is it?" Tex asked, surprised. He wasn't sure if he'd seen a copy of a guest contract.

Juan took a deep slug of the liquor.

Breck nodded. "Next thing after 'No predation.'"

"It'll grow back," Juan protested. "This is the jungle!"

"Other things might not," Breck warned him with another chuckle. "I heard Graham killed a shifter with his bare human hands, so I wouldn't so much as step off the paths the rest of this week if you want to get out of here alive."

Cowed, Juan checked his camera for damage and slunk down the path away from the bar.

"There is no end to the crazy here," Tex said, shaking his head. "I'd better get back to the bar before someone decides to go all Tom Cruise with one of the single malts."

"How's it going with your sweetheart?" Breck asked, as

they walked in through the back entrance of the bar. "Is she admitting she's your mate now that you saved her so dramatically?"

Tex could only smile foolishly at him, then he had to go mix drinks for Mr. Austria's ditzy assistant.

CHAPTER 15

*D*inners with Fred were agony.

When the restaurant was quiet and the wind was just right, Laura could hear the low thrum of Tex's laugh from the bar below and the chatter of the people enjoying his drinks and showmanship. She had to assume his antics were particularly good when there were scattered cheers and laughter.

"What do you think?" Fred asked.

Laura looked up, totally derailed on their conversation. "About?"

"I said, you should go to the swimsuit competition tonight," Fred said. "I have some paperwork I need to work on, but you should go enjoy it."

Laura pictured Tex in one of the tiny, glittery swimsuits, and had to hide her sudden flush of heat with a bite of her exquisite roasted chicken in grapes and herb sauce. She had never heard of their chef before coming to Shifting Sands, but was sure he could give any cook in the fashionable LA restaurant district a run for his money.

It suddenly occurred to Laura that if there was a big

competition tonight, maybe the bar would be slow. Slow enough for Tex to duck out.

"I think, ah, that I will turn in early tonight," she said, wondering if she could get away with feigning a yawn. "I was up really early, you know, and it was an exciting day."

Fred would think she meant the poisoning attempt, but Laura's thoughts were much more carnal, remembering the feeling of Tex's hands on her waist, the pressure of his —she stuffed another forkful of chicken in her mouth and smiled apologetically.

Two tables over, the little blonde event hostess, Jessica Linn, was protesting that her chicken was dry and tough, sending it back so stridently that conversation for several tables around her died to nothing.

"Honestly, as much as I'm paying to be here, I can't believe they don't give you more options for dinners. Seriously, the service here is deplorable."

Knowing the type, Laura suspected she was coming down off a good drunk.

"No, I don't want a replacement. If you can't cook chicken correctly, I don't want any castoffs from the buffet. I'll just hope I don't get faint from low blood sugar halfway through the swimsuit contest." She brushed Breck off with a wave of her napkin. "It's not like this is the most important event of the contest or anything. I'll just go see if anyone at the spa isn't incompetent."

She huffed away, tossing her long, bottle-blonde hair over her shoulder as she went.

Amused but hushed conversation sprang up in her wake.

"Give my regards to Chef for the meal," Laura told Breck when he checked in on them next. "I really enjoyed this."

She wondered if Chef would remember her undignified exit from his office earlier and had to smother a giggle.

Fred made one more weak attempt to convince her to watch the show, but Laura was already waving off dessert. She knew what she wanted for dessert and it wasn't any of the choices on the platter making the rounds of the dining room.

For the next hour, she paced her small hotel room. She tried concentrating on Jenny's laptop, but her mind was not up for unraveling any mysteries. She listened to the sounds of the resort through her open window instead—a note at the door of the hotel apologized for the air conditioning being under repair. Her heart lifted after a stampede of chattering traffic made its way to the theater, and the noises stilled to muffled music and distant applause.

When Tex finally knocked at the door, Laura was somehow not surprised that she knew it was him before she opened it.

It wasn't just a guess, she knew it somewhere behind her breastbone. Her wolf whined in anticipation.

She flung the door open, just as she realized that she should probably have changed into something more inviting during her wait.

Tex, holding a guitar in one hand and a cut flower in the other, looked at her as if she were wearing something that wasn't even an option from Jenny's limited wardrobe.

"I hoped you'd come," she said, breathlessly, wondering if it sounded as foolish as her smile felt.

"The bar was dead," Tex said, with a slow, appreciative smile. "I got Bastian to agree to serve drinks when the swimsuit contest breaks up and the losers need consolation drinks."

Laura grinned. "Would you like to host your own

swimsuit competition privately here this evening? I've got four designs to choose from…"

They didn't even make it to the first, as Tex put his guitar in the corner and kicked the door closed behind him, reaching for her.

Laura tipped her head back and opened her mouth, sliding her arms up around his strong neck.

This wasn't the same kind of lovemaking that they'd desperately snuck in Chef's tiny locked office. This was slower, less urgent, more controlled.

He explored her body without removing her clothing, kissing where cloth revealed her skin, but making no move to tear it off. Laura followed suit, running her hands over his chest over the staff polo shirt. She let a fingernail trace his big belt buckle and ran her hands back to squeeze his fine ass through his khaki staff pants.

They kissed and discovered each other, rising to a fever pitch of desire that Laura had never felt before.

"May I?" Tex finally asked, fingers at the bottom of her tank top.

"Oh, hell yes," Laura managed, almost past speech with craving.

He peeled her tank top off so slowly that Laura actually whimpered. Then, when her hands were tangled in the garment above her head, he held her there for a long moment, his other hand following the curve of her side with worshipful slowness.

Laura didn't exactly struggle, but gave a whine and needy wiggle, and Tex finished pulling the tanktop off of her and threw it across the room.

Laura saved him the trouble of fumbling with her bra and unclipped the back, but relished the way he pulled the straps off her shoulders and released her breasts to the cooling night air as if in slow motion.

The bra joined the tanktop across the room.

Tex stepped back. The loss of his touch was delicious torture, and Laura swayed in place.

He drank her in, all appreciation and awe, then looked her in the eyes, expression overflowing with desire.

Laura had a sudden urge to prolong this, to wind him up and make him lose control, so when he moved to touch her again, she put up a hand and drew back to sit on the bed without him.

"Let's see your moves, cowboy," she told him, and she gestured with his hand.

He gave that slow, boyish smile and reached for his hat.

"No," Laura stopped him with a word. "Leave the hat for last."

Tex tipped it at her, then proceeded to reach for his belt buckle. He flipped it open in one smooth motion, but paused, and made a show out of pulling his belt from the loops of his khakis. The cowboy boots went next, and he turned away from her so that his reach for them showed off his ass.

In one smooth move, he managed to flip off his hat, pull his shirt off over his head, and drop the hat back on. Shirtless, now wearing only a hat and his pants, he faced her again to unbutton his pants, already bulging with promise.

Laura could not believe how hot she was getting. Her nipples were hard in the evening air, and she had to shift on the bed because her pussy was hot and demanding stimulation.

He teased her with the pants, flipping them open then covering up again, in time to the distant strains of the show music. He finally unbuttoned them entirely and managed to time the release of his barely-clad cock with a distant roar of applause from the Mr. Shifter's pageant.

They had no idea what kind of a show they were missing, Laura thought.

She lifted a finger and beckoned him nearer.

He sashayed over to her obligingly, and Laura put a finger into the band of his taut briefs.

He hissed and shuddered.

"You're quite the showman," Laura said, voice warm with appreciation.

"It's not all show," Tex promised. He drew a finger of his own down Laura's shoulder and she had to suck in her breath and shiver at his touch.

Waiting was suddenly not the best option.

Laura stood and let Tex unbutton her shorts with one hand while he caressed her shoulder and side, pausing to cup her breast.

He slipped both shorts and panties down together over her ass, pausing for a squeeze. They were still for just a moment, standing close together and breathing in each other's air before he kissed her roughly and tipped her down on the bed to pull them smoothly down her legs and toss them across the room.

His weight on the bed on either side of her made it creak and if Laura could have had any thought that wasn't of his touch and his smell and his skin, it would have been gratitude that the hotel was currently deserted.

Then he was touching her eager folds and she could feel the slick wetness that had gathered during his strip-tease against his big fingers. He stroked into her, once with one finger, again with two, and she arched up and cried out in a crest of pleasure and need.

Before she could come down from it, he was stripping off his briefs and entering her. His cock filled her impossibly, then filled her more at the next stroke, each thrust feeling deeper and wider.

Laura came again, moaning and writhing in his arms, and he slowed his thrusts to ease her fall from pleasure.

When she could breathe again, she kissed him, and they were a tangle of arms and touches and mouths in waves of sensation.

When he pulled out of her, Laura felt like she'd lost something, even though she was already feeling pounded sore and had found her bliss several times. She gave a little cry, but he kissed her, then turned her on the bed and mounted her from behind.

It was a whole new range of sensation, his cock pressing in new places of joy as he slid deeper into her.

She felt it when he began to lose control, his careful thrusts becoming frantic and his hands on her arms tightening. It excited her as much as it did him and she gave a scream of release as her final orgasm outdid any of the previous, matching his own moment of climax.

His last erratic thrusts died off slowly and Laura enjoyed the spiral down as much as she had the ride up, aware again of the squeaking bed and the sounds of the evening outside the open window.

As their heartbeats finally slowed, they lay together on the bed and Tex stroked her arms and hips and sides as if he was lost in wonder.

CHAPTER 16

$\mathcal{T}$he hotel was not well insulated for sound and a few hours later, a stream of noisy chatter and stomping feet went by. Tex woke briefly, marveled at Laura, blissfully still in his arms, and went back to sleep himself.

When he woke later, the hotel was still again, but Laura was stirring in his arms and the feeling of her curves under his hands was more appealing than more sleep.

He stroked the line of her hip, the sway of her side, the cup of her breast, kissing the line of her neck as she woke.

"Well, hello Cowboy," she murmured and Tex pressed his determined member at the small of her back. They were both still naked, tangled in a single sheet together. Outside, it was raining, as it often did at night.

In darkness, they were reduced to other senses. He reveled in the silky dream of her skin, the smell of rain mixed with the heady, hot scent of her desire, and the little sounds she made when he touched her. A hand at her thigh slipped higher, curving around to appeal at more intimate places.

She moved against him, rising like a goddess over him and he could just make out the curve of her breasts in what light there was.

She encased him in one smooth move, descending on his member and raising him to some new level of sensation.

He growled in need and lust, but let her set the pace, hands on her waist, enraptured by the feeling of the curve of her hips and the way her ass met her back.

She rode him carefully, like she was testing his paces, slow, then fast, then slow in tantalizing waves.

He obliged her, meeting every stroke with a thrust of his own, until she was gasping and groaning and the cheap hotel bed was creaking like a door from a bad horror movie being played in fast forward.

Using every inch of his control, Tex saved his climax until she had gained hers, moaning and writhing on top of him.

It wasn't until he was unwinding from his own coiled knot of orgasm that he heard the pounding on the hotel wall.

Laura collapsed on him, giggling and giddy.

"Oops!" she stage-whispered near his ear.

The bed gave a last wheeze of protest as she settled beside him.

"I hope you don't get fired for disrupting the peace," she teased him.

"It would be worth it," Tex laughed back at her. "Did you really think that you could deny being my mate?" The words were out before he could stop them.

It was the first time either of them had said it aloud, and Laura's laughter stilled as her body stiffened.

"I thought I had to," she told him quietly. "I thought it

was the only way to keep my cover. You'd already met Jenny, and she might have thought you were cute, but you were definitely not her mate."

"You about drove me out of my mind," Tex had to confess. "I wasn't sure which end was up."

"I'm sorry," Laura said, but Tex felt like it was rather chilly and she was stiff in his arms.

"It couldn't have been easy," he tried to comfort her.

She sighed. "It was so hard," she confessed. "She was always the good sister, I was always the bad one who made terrible choices."

Tex pulled her closer. "You aren't *bad*," he said fiercely, his bear agreeing vehemently in his head.

"Everyone always thought I was," Laura said quietly. "If Jenny suggested something, everyone agreed. If I suggested the very same thing, my motives were always questioned, and everyone did the opposite."

"It's hard, being in the shadow of someone who seemed better," Tex agreed.

"Do you have siblings?"

Tex laughed. "An older brother who hung the moon. And probably invented sliced bread."

Tex felt Laura's laugh through his arms, rather than hearing it.

"It was pretty funny watching you trying to make sense of me," she chuckled.

"Funny?" Tex rolled over and growled near her ear. "I'll show you funny."

And he proceeded to tickle her until she was wheezing through her laughter for mercy, squirming and wiggling and jiggling in a most distracting way.

"Are you actually ready for another round?" Laura asked admiringly when she could breath again. A lazy finger traced around his erect member, getting all of his attention. "They might knock on the wall again."

"Let them," Tex said, kissing her deeply. "They can get complimentary earplugs at the spa if they want to sleep."

"I can think of better things than sleep," Laura agreed. "But I might be too sore to sit tomorrow…"

CHAPTER 17

*L*aura's plan to go swimming after lunch the next day was thwarted by a photo session at the pool.

A dozen nearly naked men were being oiled and posed, while Juan Lopez snapped orders and complained about the lighting.

"No, no! They squint, they get wrinkles! Get a shade over there!"

His mousy assistant leapt forward to scramble up on one of the tables with a gigantic white sunshade and nearly unbalanced onto the heap of men.

Mr. Canada, a brilliant red maple leaf swim brief barely covering his intimate parts, broke out of the crowd to catch the edge of the shade before it hit someone and then he paused to flex his muscles while Juan snapped a dozen extra shots, white teeth gleaming in his tanned face.

Laura was not sure her eyes could roll any harder.

Instead of joining the appreciative gawkers along the deck railing to watch the photoshoot, she wandered in through the empty bar and up the steps to the dining level.

She wasn't particularly hungry—though Tex had assured her there was no remaining poison anywhere near the kitchen, she continued to eye food with some suspicion. But having the buffet to herself was a luxury that was hard to turn down after several days of having to hold her own with her elbows to get a plate of food.

She wasn't the only one taking advantage of the brief respite from crowds.

She recognized Tex at once, more by the shape of his shoulder muscles under the staff shirt even than by the distinctive (ridiculous, she reminded herself) cowboy hat. He was filling his tray along with a collection of other staff-uniformed figures that could have given the over-groomed Mr. Shifter flock a run for their money.

She recognized Graham, the landscaper that she had witnessed frightening off a shrieking assistant with a pair of giant clippers, and Breck, the waiter who had served her the poisoned latte, as well as the lifeguard, Bastian, and another staff member whose name Laura didn't know, an exhausted-looking native man who was muddy to the knees and juggling a toolbox along with his heaping tray of food.

"Goddamn air conditioning unit for the hotel is on its last legs," he was complaining. "There's only so long I can hold it together with duct tape and bailing wire. Breck, you've got to take a look at it for me."

"If we all survive the next week, we'll have enough to get a new one," Bastian said encouragingly.

Laura was struck by the observation that he spoke as if the resort belonged to them, as if they were invested in its success. She had worked in hospitality, and she knew that it was more common for staff to be a distant subclass to the ownership. Certainly, she had never felt any kind of loyalty for her employers.

Tex turned then and Laura's full attention was caught

by the way he moved, as if he instinctively knew she was behind him, and he couldn't wait to see her. A smile was already blooming on his face, widening into a full grin at the sight of her.

Grateful that a blush wouldn't show on her brown skin, Laura strode forward boldly with her tray in hand.

The rest of the staff turned to see what Tex was looking at and gave her long, appraising looks.

What would they see? she wondered. A plump Black woman in Jenny's conservative sundress, wearing low wedge sandals? Did they believe her lawyer facade, or could they see the lies across her face?

Tex was just staring, a big smile and a slight flush on his face, so Breck stepped in. "Would you join us, Miss Smith? We'll be dining in the staff room while we have a chance and you are welcome to come eat with us."

To her surprise, the rest of the staff chimed encouragement. Even the gruff landscaper grunted and nodded at her in a fashion Laura guessed was meant to be inviting and not as terrifying as it came off.

Laura agreed, feeling uncharacteristically shy as she piled cold shrimp and fruit onto her plate. She snagged a roll so fresh it was still warm and even indulged in a rich slice of chocolate cake.

Out of sight over the railing, there was a wild cheer and appreciative hoots from the pool deck as the Mr. Shifters were cycled through their paces.

The staff room proved to be a very small room off the back of the restaurant, a round conference table in the center with a handful of chairs around it. Open windows looking out into greenery and a ceiling fan kept it from being stuffy. Tex held a chair for Laura, and she took it gingerly.

She expected to be the center of their attention, but

they all concentrated on their own trays of food and carried on easily, as if she were one of their own.

"Did you have to use the pink duct tape, Travis?" Breck asked the repairman.

"It lacks dignity," Travis replied dryly. "But it holds it together, so I'll use it."

"We're going to have to get a different distributor," Bastian said, shaking his head. "They messed up a bunch of the orders this time!"

"I think Breck ordered the pink on purpose," the landscaper said gruffly, and Laura nearly choked on her shrimp when he winked at her.

"As much as I appreciate the entire visual spectrum," Breck said severely, "I believe that duct tape should be like the force. Plain silver, dark on one side, light on the other. And it should hold the universe together."

"Geek," Bastian said, but he clearly got the reference, so Laura thought it said as much about him as it did about Breck.

They talked a little about where they were from, the invitation for Laura to join them on the table, but not full of pressure. Breck was from the midwest, Bastian was from the east coast. She was surprised to find that Travis was from a tiny town in Alaska that Laura couldn't pronounce. "Texas is cute," he said with a grin at Tex.

Tex had been gazing at Laura as he ate, and paused to glare back in good nature. Laura got the feeling that this was an old joke between them.

"What made you move to Costa Rica?" she asked Travis.

"After twenty-five Alaskan winters, you have to ask that?" he teased her easily. "I came for a winter job, but this place—Shifting Sands particularly, not just this country —gets under your skin."

Laura nodded. After only a few days, she couldn't imagine living anywhere else. She didn't think it was just Tex. She felt like this place fit her, like she clicked into a place that had been open just for her. There was something in the scent and the breeze and the way the sun hit her that felt like coming home. When she thought about fleeing further, it left an empty aching feeling, even when she fantasized about bringing Tex with her and finding another tropical place.

Her wolf, unexpectedly, agreed with her. *This is our home*, she told her firmly. *Here, with him.*

She glanced at Tex, who was trying not to be obvious about watching her while he ate.

"They're wrapping up the photoshoot." Scarlet stood in the doorway and Laura was surprised to see that she was holding her own tray of food. Scarlet felt supernatural, in a resort already full of non-human shifters, and Laura felt that it was reassuringly common of her to be eating. There was even a slice of the same chocolate cake that Laura had snagged on her tray.

The rest of the staff grumbled as they shoveled the rest of their food down as quickly as they could. Scarlet took the seat next to Laura and put down a small pile of flyers, passing one out to each of the staff. "I'd appreciate your feedback," she said, and Laura thought it sounded sincere. To her surprise, Scarlet put one in front of her.

"Looks good to me," Tex said, after a cursory look.

"Smashing," Breck agreed.

"It's glossy," Travis said, with questionable helpfulness.

The landscaper, Graham, shrugged and grunted.

Scarlet's eyes turned to her and Laura shivered at the weight of her gaze. It felt like a moment of judgment. She glanced at the flyer critically. It would be easy to say that it was fine and maybe compliment the gorgeous photographs that Scarlet had chosen.

But Laura had tasted the challenge in Scarlet's look. She read the carefully coded advertising through. A place like Shifting Sands couldn't be outright about catering to shifters—some countries gave them privileges, but more treated them like second-class citizens, others actively hunted them, and a few countries, like the US, continued to pretend they were a fairy tale. The brochure was clear that their guest-list was exclusive and only alluded to the fact that it was based on being a shifter if you read between the lines. The photograph with romping jaguars on the beach was a good clue, but it was the sort of thing that might have been just a reference to the wild jungle on the rest of the island. The flyer was all neatly deniable if it should get picked up by the wrong person.

"The kerning in the section headers is a little off. You might want to pick a different font for that," Laura said hesitantly. "And use the same one over here. You don't want to have more than two fonts in the whole thing if you can help it, one fancy, and one plain. Find a synonym for luxury or luxurious—you use it too many times in a row."

"You have some design experience," Scarlet said approvingly.

"I worked in an advertising agency for a while," Laura said. It was one of the few jobs she'd had more than a few weeks.

"They're going to be hitting the beaches soon," Bastian grumbled, draining his cup and standing.

"And the restaurant," Breck agreed with a sigh as he swallowed the last of his sandwich.

"And the bar," Tex said longingly.

Laura stood with him, glancing at the food still left on

her plate, but Scarlet said to her, "There's no need for you to rush off. Please join me to finish your lunch." Despite the 'please', it was more of a command than a request.

"Of—of course," Laura said, sitting back down. She felt automatically defensive; this was too much like being in a principal's office and she was waiting for expulsion if she said the wrong thing.

Tex hovered for a moment, clearly not sure if she needed saving or not. "I'll be working until late," he said hesitantly. "If you need anything, I'll be at the bar."

"Go on, cowboy," Laura told him with bravado. "I'll let you know if anyone tries to poison me."

His crooked smile suggested that he wasn't sure if that was a joking matter, a sentiment that Laura could agree with.

After a moment of hesitation, he bent down and put a swift kiss on her cheek. Laura only just resisted the temptation to turn and catch it on her lips. The scent of him, that close, was musky and intoxicating. Laura felt her breath catch and her heart hammer in her chest.

She watched him walk out with her appreciation for his ass tempered by the fact that Scarlet was watching both of them.

"I'd love to hear any other ideas about the resort you might have," Scarlet said, once the door had clicked behind Tex and they were alone.

Laura took another bite of mango to delay her response, savoring the fresh tang of the fruit as if it were her last. It could be. "Have you thought about allowing non-shifters in?"

Scarlet raised an eyebrow at her, but nodded at her to continue as she took a nibble of her sandwich.

"I understand you've done that for the Mr. Shifter's

competition on a temporary basis, just for the event, but you might get good business if you continued to allow shifters and their guests, whether those guests are shifters or not."

"An interesting prospect," Scarlet said, clearly considering the idea. It surprised Laura until she recalled that Scarlet thought she was Jenny; people listened to Jenny. "You are a shifter, are you not?"

"I am," Laura said automatically, then hesitated to remember that she had filled out her application stating that she wasn't. She was Jenny, she reminded herself. The *good* sister. "My father was, too, but not my mother."

"Or your sister."

Laura tried not to panic. Out of habit, she reached carefully for the nearest possible weapon, in this case a fork, and curled her fingers around it. She ignored Scarlet's words and said, as mildly as possible, "This is also the kind of place a shifter might like to have a wedding, if they could invite their human friends, too. Or kids."

"No kids," Scarlet said firmly, putting her sandwich down. "Laura, you don't need to have any fear here."

Hearing her real name from Scarlet's lips made Laura want to bolt, but she wasn't stupid enough to outright attack her with the fork now clenched in her hand. Whatever shifter animal Scarlet had within her, Laura doubted that four skinny, one-inch tines would even slow her down.

I could protect you, her wolf told her, but she didn't seem as sure as she usually was.

"Just imagine the gorgeous beach-side ceremony, and the sunset photos you could get afterwards," she babbled.

"Tex told me about your trouble."

Laura's fear transformed to fury. He'd told Scarlet? He'd jeopardized her cover by blabbing to this woman about her deepest secrets? Just like everyone else, he thought he could make better decisions for herself than she could. How *dare* he.

Scarlet continued, either oblivious to Laura's anger or assuming it was just a symptom of her fright. "I'm doubtful that your former, unsavory associates could have followed you here. We've been booked in full with a waitlist for weeks now and your visit was only just confirmed a few days prior to your arrival. I'd like to talk about the possibility that someone may have had designs on your sister and see if we can figure out any details about who this could be and how to catch them.

With effort, Laura unclenched her jaw. "I appreciate your help in this matter," she said, aware that it sounded as icy and insincere are she felt. "I don't know anyone who didn't like my sister, and I don't know anything about her work."

Scarlet gave her a long, thoughtful look, but didn't question her. "You are, of course, welcome to stay here as long as you wish, and your safety is one of our first priorities. I can arrange a room with Tex as soon as—"

"No!"

There was a moment of silence, and Scarlet cleared her throat. "Forgive me," she said formally. "I presumed that because he was your mate…"

"Being a mate apparently doesn't mean he isn't a class A jackass and I will have nothing more to do with him," Laura said without thinking. "A mate isn't a mandate."

"Very well," Scarlet said neutrally, after a heartbeat. "Your invitation to remain at Shifting Sands stands regardless of that. I will expect civility. You can come by my office and have a look at my standard contract at any time. It's room and board with profit share instead of tips and you would be expected to pull your weight; no one is too good for laundry duty or cleaning when it's needed."

Laura wondered if she imagined the skepticism in her voice, but it only hardened her resolve.

Don't fall for cowboys, she told herself. *You knew better.*

She always knew better and fell anyway.

CHAPTER 18

*T*ex flipped the bottle in one hand, a grin the size of Texas on his face while he tossed the shaker in the other hand. He poured the concoction out with a flourish and added the garnish with a spin.

The scattered applause warmed his heart, but not as much as the memory of Laura in his arms. It was her smile that he remembered the best. Her curves, yes, and oh little green gods, the way she rose to meet him… but it was the relaxed, easy smile that lit up her face afterwards that made him feel like he'd just turned a stampede.

"A gin and tonic, Cowboy! And a Libertas!"

Tex tipped his hat at the bikini-clad guest, putting the beer glass under the tap while he selected the gin from the glass display behind him and put ice in a tumbler. A generous splash and a squirt from the tonic tap and he had both drinks out on napkins.

He turned to take the next order and found himself looking at Laura's face.

It was not smiling. It was neither relaxed, nor easy.

His bear actually quailed at that face, filled with anger and looking for a fight.

Tex immediately cast back to try to figure out what on earth he had done wrong. They had parted amicably, as far as he knew. She'd joked about an attempt to poison her again. Had someone actually tried to? Had he failed to protect her?

We would not fail, his bear insisted.

"What's wrong?" Tex blurted. "You look…" angry probably assumed too much "…upset?" He had a feeling careful word choice was going to be important here.

"Upset?" Laura said, with icy tones. "I look upset?"

It's a trap, his bear helpfully told him.

Tex swallowed. "Yes?"

"What an amazing coincidence," Laura said sarcastically. "I am upset," she continued. "I am livid. I am furious. I just came by to tell you not to bother coming by tonight. Or any night."

She turned on her heel and stalked away, heels clicking on the tiled floor. Tex watched her go with his jaw hanging, divided between his instincts telling him to follow her and his duty to stay at the bar.

"Can I get a beer?" a guest asked from the end of the bar.

"Margarita!" someone called.

Bastian, still in his lifeguard gear, saved him from the dilemma by walking up at that moment. It was just getting dark and he was getting off his watch.

"Go get her," the dragon shifter said in a resigned voice, coming behind the bar. Clearly, he had heard Laura's departure. A gaggle of guests already nursing their drinks were staring and murmuring about it as well. "I can mix up some sidecars and spill some beer in a cup with the best of them."

"Thank you," Tex said, heartfelt. "I owe you one."

"You and everyone," Bastian said, rolling his eyes. He wasn't as cranky as he had been, now that they had settled into the new house, but he wasn't entirely back to his usual cheerful self, either.

Tex didn't pause, but took off after Laura, who had left through the back entrance towards the hotel.

He caught her almost at the hotel door and took her arm.

"Laura, Laura, love…" he said, glancing around to make sure no one was in obvious earshot.

"Don't you Laura, Laura, love me," she snapped back, shaking her arm free. "*That* is why I am *upset*. You can't keep your mouth shut with the one secret I give you. You betrayed me. You told, well at least Scarlet, and probably half the big-mouthed staff."

Tex stood his ground, but relinquished her arm. "I had to tell Scarlet," he protested. He hadn't really thought about the fact that he was betraying her trust, but he'd known that Scarlet could help protect her and that knowing the truth would help her do that. His mate's safety was his first, driving priority.

"You don't get to choose for me," Laura spat. "I make my own choices, Tex."

"This isn't a choice," Tex said firmly.

"Everything is a choice," Laura retorted. "And I can choose not to be with someone who can't respect my secrets."

"You're my mate," Tex insisted.

"And what, being my mate makes you my owner? You get to make my decisions for me?" Laura scoffed. "I pick my path and that may not include you, Cowboy, so don't get too settled."

The idea cut to the center of Tex's chest and he was

suddenly, desperately afraid that he'd screwed this up and had no idea how to fix it.

She was turning to walk away into the hotel when there was suddenly a muffled bang above them, followed by a very familiar panicked woman's scream and the wail of the smoke alarm.

"That sounded like it came from my hotel room," Laura said in a small voice, casting Tex a wide-eyed look.

Laying aside their argument, they ran for the stairs.

CHAPTER 19

The hallway at the top floor had a little smoke that smelled to Laura like plastic but there didn't appear to be any fire. Laura's hotel door was open and several guests were milling about outside of it, peering in. She wondered briefly what the smoke smelled like to Tex's keen nose, then elbowed her way into her hazy room past the housekeeping cart.

Marie was sobbing in the arms of Juan Lopez, who was trying to comfort her.

"I barely touched it," Marie wailed. "I was just dusting up, and bang!"

Her desk was blackened, along with the curtains nearby and the ceiling above. The mangled wreck of Jenny's precious laptop was shattered plastic and warped, exposed circuit boards. The paper stationery on the desk had burned away and the cover of the 3-ring binder of resort details had melted into a grotesque puddle. The scene was smothered in a fine pale dust and there was a fire extinguisher on its side by Juan's feet. The fire alarm continued to wail.

"What is going on here?"

Laura wasn't even sure how Scarlet had gotten there; she hadn't been in the stairwell with them, but now she was right behind Tex, edging past the housekeeping cart into the room.

"We just got here," Tex told her, as Marie protested, "I barely touched it!"

"My laptop," Laura said weakly, and Juan scoffed, "I don't know what kind of place this is!"

The fire alarm was still shrieking.

"Enough!" Scarlet said, holding up her hand.

Marie buried her face in Juan's chest with a squeak but the fire alarm, to Laura's wry surprise, did not silence at her command.

"Tex, go turn off the alarm."

Tex, beside Laura, stiffened and Laura thought he was going to protest, then he agreed, "Can't hear yourself think this way." To Laura he said, "I'll be right back."

Laura didn't have time to tell him it was irrelevant to her. For such a big man, he certainly moved quickly.

Scarlet pointed at Juan. "You, explain."

Juan drew himself up, facing the challenge in Scarlet's voice. "I was walking past when I heard the explosion and the scream. The door was open and I went in to find the desk on fire. I used the fire extinguisher to put out the flames just as the smoke detector went off."

"He saved my life!" Marie added at that point.

"Are you hurt?" Scarlet asked Marie briskly.

Marie shook her head vigorously, remaining in the protective circle of Juan's arms. "No," she said in a trembling voice. "I barely touched it," she repeated. "I was just dusting."

Scarlet frowned at the desk and picked up a sooty pen

that had rolled to the ground. "This isn't how laptops usually fail," she said dryly.

The fire alarm abruptly went still and the silence seemed remarkable.

"Clearly this is another attempt on Miss Smith's life," Juan announced into the space it left.

Laura had been looking in despair at the black disaster of the laptop. All of her memories of Jenny were there.

But at Juan's statement, she looked up and the enormity of the situation crashed down on her.

Someone really was trying to kill her. And it was more the cartel's style to slit throats in sleep, not poison lattes and blow up laptops. Someone else was after her. Or after Jenny.

"Jenny? Jenny?" Fred pushed into the room through the growing crowd, panting and sweating. "Are you okay? Oh, Jenny, what happened?"

Juan was happy to repeat his tale of heroics for him while Scarlet thoughtfully took pictures on her phone of the mess. Tex returned during the tale, to find there was no space in the tiny hotel room for him to squeeze in. Laura was equal parts glad to see him sulk at the doorway and sorry not to have him at her side; Fred was a disappointing replacement and, even though she was furious with Tex, she felt safer with him at her side than with Fred.

"What were you doing cleaning the hotel room so late?" Fred asked Marie suspiciously.

Marie, who had finally stopped crying, burst into tears again. "I couldn't get all the rooms done any earlier!"

Scarlet swooped to her defense at once. "We are all working odd shifts right now. The Mr. Shifter event has left us spread thin."

Juan sniffed and muttered something barely audible about being under-staffed and unprepared. Scarlet shot him an unappreciative look and he snapped his mouth shut.

"Are you okay?" Fred asked Laura again. He was rubbing her arm in a familiar way, and even though she knew that Jenny wouldn't have, Laura pushed him away with a growl.

"I'm fine," she insisted. "I wasn't even here."

"Your poor laptop," Fred said. "Did you have much that wasn't backed up?"

"No," Laura lied. "I have *everything* I need on the cloud."

Jenny would do that.

Scarlet turned to Laura decisively. "You can't stay here tonight," she said firmly. "Tex..."

Laura was about to stop her, but Scarlet only told him, "Get Travis and find every free fan that you can to get the smoke in the hallway cleared out."

Tex looked at Laura, who ignored him, before agreeing. "Yes, Ma'am." He vanished back into the audience.

Scarlet turned her scowl to them next. "There's nothing more to see here, people." They scattered obediently, chattering excitedly as they went.

To Juan she said, "Thank you for your quick thinking."

"He's my hero," Marie said, still tangled around him.

He looked pleased, if not quite sure what to do with the housekeeper clinging to him. "It was my pleasure," he finally said, and took Scarlet's hint to leave, Marie trailing alongside him.

The door shut behind them and Laura and Scarlet were alone in the little room, which felt much larger with everyone gone.

"Pack up your personal items, but leave your clothing," Scarlet commanded. "We'll launder everything to get the smoke smell out and bring it to the cottage I'll put you up in. It's on the rustic side, the shower is outside and only has cold water, but it's the last unoccupied room we have and it will do in a pinch. I'll see about replacing the laptop, of course, and I'll be placing a guard on you at all times."

Scarlet did not so much as hint that Laura room with Tex, which she was grateful for, and Laura knew better than to argue about a guard at this point.

"Thank you," she said weakly.

"I'll wait in the hallway while you get your things together," Scarlet said gently.

Alone in the hotel room, Laura wandered about aimlessly for a moment, putting things randomly in her carry-on bag. She stared at the burnt-up laptop and tried to imagine what she was going to do next. Most of her wanted to sit down on the extinguisher-dusted bed and sob her eyes out, but she was afraid that if she started, she would never stop.

So she shouldered her bag and went out to let Scarlet lead her on.

CHAPTER 20

*T*ex finished out the night at the bar in a stupor. He didn't have the energy for any stunts and had to ask people to repeat their orders more times than he had ever had to in his life.

Laura's flashing eyes and bared teeth were burned into his brain. His bear, always a blustery, self-confident brute he had to restrain, was as shocked and dismayed as he was and offered no help.

She doesn't want us? His bear was crushed.

Had he done what she accused him of? Had he betrayed her trust? It simply hadn't occurred to him *not* to tell Scarlet the truth. At the best of times, he was a miserable liar and there was something about Scarlet that made falsehood feel pointless. Besides, his first priority was Laura's protection and Scarlet was her best hope of that, next to him.

Not that he'd been able to help her today.

"I asked for a beer like ten minutes ago," Mr. Canada groused. Tex stared at him stupidly while the girl hanging on his arm tittered drunkenly.

"Sorry, sir," Tex said automatically. "What kind was that?"

"A pilsner," Mr. Canada scoffed. The girl giggled again.

Tex looked at the clock, which seemed to be crawling towards closing time too slowly and poured the beer more sloppily than he usually did, requiring him to mop up the counter afterwards.

Mr. Canada was unimpressed. "Americans," he said scornfully to his armcandy as they moved away from the bar to one of the tables overlooking the pool.

Her silly laugh made Tex long for Laura's intelligent, warm chuckle.

But... she doesn't want us? Tex sometimes thought that his bear was not the swiftest animal that could have shared his head.

She will, Tex replied to him, not entirely convinced himself. *She has to.*

He tried not to think too hard about the fact that he'd always considered himself unlucky in love... and that maybe that really was the truth.

The cottage that Travis had put Laura up in was at the very edge of the jungle, nearly swallowed in vines and flowers. The path was an obstacle course of old concrete fractured by roots, not yet replaced with white gravel like the rest of the updated paths.

Tex wandered there directly following last call and nearly lost his hat to one of the overhanging branches.

Graham was sitting on the lowest front step, a menacing shadow with a machete, but when Tex approached, he stood up. They exchanged a look that didn't require words and Graham shrugged and left Tex to take his vigil.

Tex mauled his hat in his hands as he stood at the doorstep, but didn't knock.

Finally, he simply sat where Graham had been.

He could no more push himself on her than he could leave her unprotected. Her doorstep was the best place for him, for now.

CHAPTER 21

$\mathcal{L}$aura didn't sleep until Tex arrived.

She sensed him changing places with the surly landscaper and spent several long moments anticipating the knock on the door before she realized he wasn't going to.

It was strange to be courted by someone who listened to her refusals, who treated her with respect.

Once she figured out that he planned to stay the night on her doorstep, she fell easily into a deep, restful sleep. Her dreams were of a strange field of tall grass, brightly lit as if by daylight, but the sky had no sun.

The cottage had not been fitted with curtains or blinds, so the rising sun woke her early. She looked at it curiously for several moments, trying to recall the details of the fleeting dream.

Laura dressed in the same sundress she had been wearing the night before and went out onto the front porch to find a gigantic brown bear that took up not a step, but all the steps, head laying on crossed paws next to a tidy pile of Tex's clothing topped by his ridiculous hat. He sat up when she came out, moving aside so she could get down the stairs.

He is a fine bear, her wolf told her suggestively.

He is a fine man, she responded with a sigh.

Instead of walking past, she sat down beside him. She ought to be afraid, she thought. Each of his paws was the size of her head, fringed with sharp claws as long as her fingers.

"My secrets are mine to keep," she said severely. "I choose who to share them with, not you. I get to decide how to keep myself safe."

The bear gave a whine, then shifted gracefully down to the form of a man sitting beside her. A gorgeous man.

A gorgeous, very naked man.

And to Laura's surprise, the gorgeous, naked man did not offer a single excuse. He could have pointed out, rightfully, that Scarlet would probably have figured it out anyway, or that he needed her help to protect her.

All he said was, "It was wrong of me. I am sorry."

Laura waited, too experienced with men not to expect the 'but...'

It didn't come.

"You won't always be able to protect me," Laura pointed out.

His sorrowful look cut her to the heart. "I can always try," he said fiercely. "I couldn't rest if you weren't safe."

Laura picked up his hat, running a finger along the band before setting it on her head. It was big on her, but she had enough hair to hold it up from her eyes.

"I know you meant well," she conceded. "I'm not used to having someone willing to run to my rescue," she confessed. "I'm not sure what to do with it."

"I like you in that hat," Tex said shyly, with a crooked smile.

Laura tipped it at him, an echo of his own habits. "Pleased ta meetcha," she drawled.

"I am so glad I met you," Tex said, all sincerity and chivalry.

Laura gave a laugh that was more snort. "Me, with all of my baggage."

"Ma'am," Tex said seriously, "I'm happy to carry all of your baggage."

Laura tipped forward to kiss him, forgetting that his hat was still on her head. It hit him in the forehead and he lifted it off her head in one smooth motion, cupping her face with his big, gentle hands.

She had not forgotten that he was naked, however hard she was trying to ignore it. Her whole body tingled to be so close to him, and she put one of her hands on his chest. Fine hair curled over her sepia fingers. He felt like the softest leather imaginable, warm in the early sun.

He shivered at her touch and drew her in for another, deeper kiss.

They kissed until they had to break apart for breath, hands exploring over muscles and the planes of their bodies. Tex had his hand up under her sundress, barely touching the wet heat of her entrance, while she just accidentally brushed the attentive member that Tex was sporting. And kept accidentally brushing it.

"Scarlet wants you to take the boat to the mainland, Tex. Travis can't go because he is fixing the toilet in cottage eight."

The voice that interrupted them was matter-of-fact and Laura and Tex scrambled apart hastily to find a woman standing in the overgrown path, looking at them with open curiosity. Her salt-and-pepper hair was wild around her face and her feet were bare beneath a short, flowing sundress.

"Gizelle," Tex said, strangled. He pulled his hat over his lap. "This is Laura."

Gizelle stared at Laura. "Your skin is much browner than mine," she said candidly.

Laura blinked at her unexpected statement, and slowly agreed, "Yes, it is." Gizelle had pale, freckled skin and Laura couldn't decide if she looked very young, with her straight, innocent gaze, or very old, with the white that streaked her hair and the unexpected wariness in her expression.

Tex coughed. "Gizelle hasn't been in human form very long," he explained, hinting at a deeper story.

Gizelle finally turned her intense stare from Laura to Tex and she felt like she could breathe again. "Scarlet says we need more things before the bonfire tonight and Travis wants duct tape that isn't pink. I like the pink duct tape. Chef wants strawberries, twenty pounds if you can get them. What were you doing when I walked up?"

Laura blessed the brown skin that kept the heat of embarrassment from showing. Tex, not so lucky, was scarlet-faced. The blush extended down to his chest, Laura was amused to see.

"I'll explain it to you later," Tex promised. He stood up and grabbed his pile of clothing, keeping the hat in place in front of him. "I'll just go grab a quick shower…"

He paused just a few strides down the path. "Do you want to come to the mainland with me?"

Laura had to consider only a moment—escape from the crowded resort in a boat with only Tex?—and she said, "Yes!" exactly as Gizelle primly said, "No, thank you."

The two women looked at each other and Gizelle

explained, "Scarlet says I shouldn't, until I stay human when I get frightened. You'll have a nice trip. The sunlight will be pouring before the ocean gets in."

"How long will it take you to get ready?" Tex asked Laura.

Laura shrugged. It wasn't like she spent a lot of time on makeup and the shower was too chilly to tempt her to stay in it long. She did want a quick bite first, though. "Thirty minutes?"

"You know the staff house by the cliffs? The one closest to the beach?" At Laura's nod, Tex said, "Meet me there when you're ready to go."

Then he left and once his adorable bare buttcheeks had vanished around the corner, Gizelle turned to Laura.

"Will *you* explain what you were doing?" she asked directly.

Laura felt her cheeks heat again. "He's my mate," she finally said, simply.

"Ah," Gizelle said knowingly.

Laura braced herself to explain further, but Gizelle tossed her head as if she were scenting the air and said, "He likes you," before she turned and scampered off.

Probably, her befuddled look was similar to the look Fred gave her when she caught him leaving the buffet. "I'm headed to the mainland on the boat today," she told him. "So don't worry if you don't see me around!" Then she was off to grab the quickest food available at the buffet before she went to meet Tex.

Laura wasn't sure what to expect when she tapped at the door to the staff house, but it definitely wasn't the cheerful roar of welcome that the staff gave her.

"Come in!" Breck hollered from the kitchen. "*Mi* castle, *es so* castle, or something! Can I get you a breakfast beer? Some juice?"

Travis stood at the bottom of the stairs and shouted up, "Tex, your *girlfriend* is here!" He wandered back into the kitchen to take a plate of eggs from Breck. "It's supposed to be *mi casa*, my *house*."

"Compared to our last place, this is totally a castle," Breck retorted. "It's also one of the only buildings in the place with its own kitchen. Do you want some eggs Miss Smith?"

Bastian, who had answered the door, smiled down at her. "We're watching last night's speeches, join us?" He was already wearing his lifeguard's uniform, the first aid kit strapped to his waist.

Even Graham thawed enough to smile and stand up to remove a pile of questionable literature from the end of the loveseat so she could sit.

Laura did sit, gingerly, and accepted the juice Breck brought her with a flourish.

The Mr. Shifter competition being streamed on the big TV was returning from a promotional break and the little blonde hostess was standing in front of the red curtains of the little theatre, all her charm turned on. If Laura hadn't watched her stridently return a perfectly good meal at the restaurant two nights before, she might have believed the charismatic little act.

Mr. India took the stage and flashed a perfect white smile before launching into a well-rehearsed tirade about responsibility to the environment.

"Keep it down," Breck told Tex, as he stomped down the stairs in his cowboy boots. "This one's actually coherent."

"Unlike Mr. Canada, who might have written his speech from a Tim Hortons menu. Maple syrup and donuts, eh?" Travis was clearly unimpressed.

The bachelor banter faded to Laura's ears at the sight of Tex. Mr. India, in his crisp white shirt, was forgotten.

Cowboys had never done it for her, but there was something about Tex, something that made Mr. India look inconsequential. It was something that made Laura forgive the foolish boots and the big buckle. And the hat was perfect.

"Bring me back some double A batteries, will you, Tex?" Travis indicated an ancient personal tape player.

"I need a new pair of socks," Breck showed off the hole in his stockinged toe. "And can you grab me copy of the latest People magazine?"

"A new septic system would be great," Travis quipped. "I don't know how this one hasn't failed yet."

"We've only got a few more days," Tex reminded them calmly. "Tonight are the final awards, we just have to get through the,m and then the beach party, and almost everyone will be leaving tomorrow on the charter."

"I don't know if the water system is going to last that long," Travis said. His golden skin couldn't hide the dark circles under his eyes. As early as it was, Laura suspected he had been up late the night before and already been hard at work that morning.

"I wish I was going," he added longingly. "But I know if I step foot off the island, there won't be a working gener-ator in the place."

"I could probably fix a generator," Breck told him. "But I am not touching the toilets, so you aren't allowed to go."

"If people wouldn't keep flushing whatever the hell they are flushing, they'd all work just fine," Travis stormed. "Seriously, who flushes paper towels?"

"Let's get out of here before Travis goes off on a rant

about the crappy electrical system that the original builders put in," Tex suggested at Laura's elbow.

"Lucky dog!" Breck called after them.

The dock at the south end of the beach was simple and old, which also described the boat that waited for them. It had two outboards, one tipped up out of the water. While the boat was still moored and Laura was getting comfortable in her seat, Tex drew the other up and put the dry one into service. "Travis says to switch them every time we use them," he explained to Laura's quizzical look. "Says it prolongs their life."

"Why are there two?" Laura asked.

"Emergency, mostly, but also speed. It's a good hour to get to the mainland, a good hour back, and it's open water. You can run both if you're in a hurry, but it's really loud that way, and we're in no rush."

One engine sounded plenty loud to Laura; it drowned out easy conversation as it was.

The day was beautiful; Gizelle's lyrical description of pouring sunshine seemed incredibly accurate. The ocean glittered under the rays and twice they saw pods of whales in the distance, flipping tails and blowing spouts. Laura would not have wanted to see them closer.

"Otter!" Tex pointed out. A small dark head swam beside them for a short while, but they quickly outstripped it. "You don't often see just one of them," Tex observed.

Laura let her hand trail in the sparkling waves and marveled at the ocean. It was incredibly clear. At first, they could see down through turquoise layers to the sand and reef below, but it fell away to unspeakably dark depths very quickly.

There was something comfortable about the journey; the rocking of the boat was initially alarming, but it settled into a soothing, mesmerizing pattern. They felt like a part of it, like they fit together into an interlocking destiny.

Turning to look behind them, Laura watched the island shrink. Roofs and landmarks that already felt like home disappeared into the dark emerald jungle that surrounded it and eventually even that dissolved into the waves of the ocean. It was an odd feeling of loss when it was finally impossible to make out. But by that time, the mainland was in sight, stretching across the eastern horizon like an invitation.

Tex took the boat into a protected little jetty, to a dock so rickety it made the Shifting Sands dock look new and modern. The mix of boats already there ranged from shining yachts to tiny rowboats with ancient outboards bungee-corded onto them.

"Can we just leave the boat here?" Laura asked, looking around. The village they'd landed at was a curious mix, the kind of abject poverty she'd expect from a third world nation directly next to a shiny new tourist cart with a menu in English, German, and Japanese.

"It's perfectly safe," Tex assured her. "They know us here, and no one will risk Scarlet's wrath by stealing anything. That's the sort of thing that only happens once..."

He helped her up onto the dock, which swayed under their steps, and laughed and held her up when Laura's sea legs caught her by surprise. "It didn't feel like that long of a ride," she laughed.

"We'll put our order in at Lee's and go have lunch and a cold drink while they get it together," Tex suggested, tucking her arm into his and strolling to solid ground.

Lee's seemed to be a poorly marked shack from the outside, but was a modern grocery on the inside, stacked to the low ceiling with Spanish-marked goods and more bottled water than Laura had seen in her life. Tex went straight to the back, where a grizzled little Asian man took their order.

"Not sure I can get that many bottles together," Lee said, shaking his head over the wine order. "But I'll ask Lita to run up to the In and Out and see what they have."

Tex tipped his hat to him. "My thanks, sir."

"Anytime, Cowboy. Take your beautiful young lady here over to the market for a while and come back late afternoon. We'll have your boat loaded by four."

Tex shook his hand.

"Give my regards to Ms. Scarlet," Lee added with a wink.

"Always," Tex agreed.

"They know Scarlet here?" Laura observed. "I didn't think she left the island."

"I've stopped being surprised by anything to do with Scarlet," Tex said.

"Will we be able to get back before dark?" Laura asked with sudden concern. She didn't like the idea of boating out into darkness without being able to see where they were going. She was honestly a little unnerved by the thought of boating on the open ocean altogether, but she didn't want to admit that to Tex.

"When Lee says four, that means four on the dot, so we'll have a little over an hour to get back before sunset. Should be fine."

The reassurance was all Laura needed to enjoy herself.

They ate lunch at a place on the outskirts of the village that was mostly a leaning porch and a hut, but it served ice cold colas in glass bottles and plates piled with rice, beans, plantains, a salsa Tex introduced as *picadillo*, something that was almost coleslaw but not quite, and a thigh of spicy grilled chicken.

A skinny stray dog made itself at home underneath their table, and Laura fed it the last of her rice when she was too full for the last few mouthfuls.

There was something about the hum of the ocean and the insects, the cries of toucans in the treetops. The fruity smell of warm jungle was comfortable, and the hum of conversation that Laura didn't understand somehow didn't make her feel excluded. Everyone flashed wide, sincere smiles at her, eyes almost crinkled shut in their enthusiasm.

Laura had stuffed herself full and the stray dog was thumping its grateful tail on her foot when Tex stood up and took her hand. "Let's go see the market."

The market proved to be a crooked row just off the beach of tents and cars with their back hatches open, an informal collection of local merchants selling an array of colorful goods. Scarves fluttered in the breeze and opportunistic sellers offered overpriced suntan lotion and bottled water next to hand-carved masks and sculptures.

Tex stepped knowingly into a slightly more permanent booth, built of weathered plywood on two sides, with a metal roof over tables heaped with open bins of spices.

"I've got a shopping list from Chef," he said apologetically. "I thought I'd get it out of the way first."

"Don't mind me," Laura said, and Tex entered heated negotiations for quantities of spice in the pounds.

Laura wandered away to let him haggle, stroking silky sarongs hung in wild-colored clusters at the edge of the next booth.

"Real silk," the vendor tried to tempt her.

Laura stopped touching them and moved on with an apologetic smile and shrug. The vendor moved on to the tourist behind her, launching at once into a friendly explanation of the dying technique.

Laura glanced to find that Tex and the spice seller were still deep in discussion and wandered to the next booth.

It had a collection of carnival masks, brilliantly painted and finely detailed. She was used to masks that relied on the natural color of the wood, but these were entirely covered in a rainbow of paint, bright animal markings, with tiny toucans and many-hued parrots added in relief along the edges. An empty-eyed wildcat with a tiny emerald island painted on its forehead caught Laura's attention.

"Hand-carved by my uncle, painted by my sister," the seller said with an ingratiating smile. "A special price for you."

Laura touched it gingerly, drawn to it but skeptical of the sales pitch. The price tag was on the high end of reasonable, but even reasonable was out of her price range.

She pulled her fingers back, sobering to remember that she was going to need every penny she had in the event she needed to flee further. The idea of staying at Shifting Sands was undeniably appealing, but part of her still doubted her safety there. There had been two attempts on her life, and although Scarlet was skeptical that it was the mob, Laura couldn't imagine what else it might be.

And she couldn't fathom the idea of someone wanting to hurt Jenny.

She shook her head at the hopeful seller, and walked on, past rows of magnets and souvenirs that had COSTA RICA written in all caps, and, almost as frequently, "*Pura Vida*," the Costa Rican motto that meant "pure life."

She was looking at carved wooden keychains when she glanced around and saw a fit, dark-haired young man in obviously American clothing talking to the seller in the next booth. He looked shifty, with his close-mouthed smile and mirrored sunglasses. Did she imagine the words "Shifting Sands" at the edge of her hearing? She ducked her head and turned away from them. How far would she have to run to get away from the cartel? And how would she do it with the paltry money she had?

She hurried back to where Tex, a heavy bag of spices already purchased, was haggling for socks and double A batteries with a seller out of the back of his car.

A glance back showed the young man buying a keychain, laughing easily. He looked like a tourist, not like a hitman. Laura shook her head and steadied her breath.

There was no point in becoming paranoid.

She greeted Tex with a smile that was first forced, then irresistible in return for his delighted grin. Something about his boyish charm drove away her dark musings, and she resolved not to return to them until they were back on the island. She would enjoy this excursion.

The vendor, having lost Tex's attention, made a valiant effort to get it back. "Both for twenty-five hundred colon, perhaps?"

Tex looked back at him blankly, their negotiations clearly forgotten. "Sure," he laughed with a shrug.

Laura hoped she hadn't distracted him into a terrible price.

Money exchanged, Tex took Laura's hand and they walked on, pausing to look at the items for sale.

Tex convinced her to model ridiculous gemstone sunglasses from one table. Laura got him back by convincing him to try on a rainbow sombrero.

"I love it," she teased, hiding his cowboy hat behind her back. "It's your fabulous new look. Much better than the cowboy hat!"

Tex laughed at her, reaching for his own hat, but Laura giggled and held it away.

Tex tossed the sombrero back onto the display and made a tackle for Laura, tickling her until she released the hat, and then refused to let go of her without a kiss, which she willingly gave him.

When she glanced back towards the market, she thought she saw the man with the mirrored sunglasses, but he disappeared back into the crowd before she could be sure.

CHAPTER 22

"*A*re you going to want dinner before we head back?" Tex asked Laura.

"After that lunch? I don't want a whole meal," Laura laughed.

Tex loved the way her eyes sparkled when she wasn't worrying about her future. He would have done anything in the world to keep that stress from her beautiful face. He vowed to make it his life's goal to make her laugh whenever she wasn't.

He introduced her to *queso palmito*, the mild string cheese ball that peeled into delicious layers, and paired it with roadside strawberries.

"Oh," Laura said with delight, putting a second berry to her lips. "These are the best strawberries I've ever had."

She tried to pay the vendor, but there was no way Tex was going to let her open her wallet. "My mother raised me right," he told her firmly.

The stubborn flash in her eyes told him he was in for a fight, but a moment of darkness passed over her face and she put her wallet back in her purse instead.

They walked in silence down to the edge of the beach. A downed tree made the perfect bench, and they sat with feet in the sand, watching the wild brown children playing in the waves. A few tourists in designer chairs sat with a big cooler between them. Laughter and chatter made a lovely soundtrack to their little snack and Tex snuck his hand into Laura's. It lightened his heart when she squeezed it and leaned into him.

Putting his arms around her was the most natural, perfect way to sit.

"I love you," he said, so quietly that he wasn't sure if she heard him. She didn't respond.

After they had licked their hands clean, Tex glanced at his cracked phone display. "They've probably got our order packed up at the boat," he said reluctantly. "We'll want to get out soon to make it back before dark."

He stood and offered a hand to Laura. She looked at it skeptically for a moment, then gave him a slow smile and let him help her up. Tex shouldered the dense spice package and settled his hat on his head, tucking Laura's hand into the crook of his elbow.

They walked back over the sand, laughing at the tiny crabs that scuttled away from their steps, and peering up into the sun at the calling seabirds.

Their steps slowed as they reached the pier and they found that the boat was indeed ready to go. The delivery boy, hauling an empty wagon bigger than he was, presented them with a receipt that Tex signed off on. He put the carbon copy into his wallet and then turned to help Laura step down into the boat, to find that she had already scrambled into her seat.

They putted out of the little bay slowly, then Tex kicked the motor into high gear and the boat skipped over the little waves easily. The sun only just seemed to be dipping down from the zenith, but Tex knew how fast it could set. He squinted out onto the horizon, but the island was still invisible. After a moment of consideration, he crawled back into the stern of the boat and went through the steps to put the second engine into service.

At Laura's quizzical look, he explained, "We want to get back before dark and we're just cutting it a little close."

The engine tipped easily down into the water and Tex pulled out the choke and yanked on the starter cord until it caught. The motor thrummed to life, coughed, and then caught in earnest.

He was happier with the speed they were making after that.

"Here!" he told Laura, pulling her into his lap. He showed her how to steer the ship, and let her find the right combination of throttle to use against the wave, and how to point the compass.

She grinned and squeaked when she mistimed her charge against a wave, sending shattered saltwater over them. Tex held a protective arm around her, enjoying the way she reacted to the ocean by moving in his lap.

He kissed the back of her neck, and she responded with a throaty purr. "You'll make me drive the boat off course," she scolded him.

Tex was giving her another kiss, followed by an irresistible nibble, when the second engine gave a sudden, unexpected sputter and roar. He only had time to turn and look at it curiously before it exploded.

CHAPTER 23

*L*aura was trying to focus on keeping the tiny jumping compass line on track with the distraction of Tex's mouth at the back of her neck. She barely heard the noise of the explosion over the roar of the ocean and the engine and she was caught by surprise when Tex's arms wrapped around her and pulled her out of the chair and over the side of the boat.

The water was shocking, even if it wasn't exactly cold, and Laura thrashed reactively when she came up again— until a chunk of railing flew over her head and she realized that Tex was trying to pull her away from the sinking, burning boat, one of his arms around her. For a moment, she went limp, and Tex's strong strokes drew her away from the blaze. Then she added her own strength to their retreat, as the fire hit the water and turned to explosive steam. The boat gave a death gurgle as it sank, and the sound of it was lost to the endless ebb and splash of the ocean around them.

Laura kicked off her shoes and tread water beside Tex,

who had only reluctantly let her go to remove his own boots.

"What the hell was that?" she demanded.

Tex shook his head in confusion. "I have no idea what happened!"

His hat was gone, Laura realized with a pang, and she never expected that she would miss it so badly.

Debris surrounded them: chunks of decking, engine molding, a large piece of the awning. Her purse had probably sunk like a stone, but Laura suddenly remembered Jenny's phone, still in her shorts pocket. She'd bought one of those ridiculous waterproof cases for it, but she'd only hoped to save it from being splashed at the beach; she wasn't sure if it was going to work for a full-body salt-water soak.

She must have looked awkward, treading water with one arm and reaching for it with the other. A wave hit her square in the mouth while her attention was divided and she spat and sputtered.

The swells that seemed insignificant in a boat were far more malevolent when Laura barely had her head above water.

While she struggled with her soaking pocket underwater, Tex swam into the debris, testing various pieces with his weight. They weren't going to be able to tread water until someone found them, and swimming back to the mainland seemed as impossible as swimming to the island —both were tiny on the horizon.

Laura was alarmed to see that the sky was beginning to tint red as the sun began its madcap decent for the ocean.

"What the tarnation?!" It was as close to swearing as Laura had heard from Tex, and she looked up from her successful retrieval of the phone to see a small whiskered face poking from the water between them, not even an arms length away.

The otter chittered at her anxiously while Laura backpedaled in alarm.

As quickly as it appeared, it dove down again out of sight, little tail flipping behind it on the choppy water.

It came up a stone's throw away, chattered noisily, and then dove again, to reappear further out.

"It's probably scared of us," Laura guessed.

It scolded them, then made an unmistakable gesture with its diminutive paw, almost capsizing itself with the effort.

"It... wants us to follow it?"

Lacking any other guidance, Laura and Tex exchanged a helpless look and kicked out after it.

It led them unerringly to a chunk from the bow of the boat.

"I thought dolphins were the ones that were supposed to do deep sea saving," Laura said. "I've never heard of otters doing anything like this."

"I think we could sit on that," Tex said, testing its buoyancy by pulling on the edge.

He helped Laura clamber aboard first, a strong hand on her rear nothing but professional.

Laura still found it incredibly sexy.

She moved carefully to the far side of the wreckage to balance it as Tex pulled himself up.

It was tippy and water sloshed up over it regularly, but they could huddle together near the center and catch their breath, at least. Tex's strong arm around her helped Laura calm her racing heart and she let her head rest at his shoulder.

"Couldn't ask for a more romantic view," Tex said, in his dear drawl.

The sun was plunging for the water and all of the waves around them were crimson and gold, glittering with a million facets in every direction. The sky above them was a tapestry of color, rich purple scattered with puffy orange and magenta clouds.

"I think I'd prefer the view from the beach," Laura laughed, but she had to appreciate the incredible hues.

She was acutely aware that they had just survived something awful, that they were stranded on a shard of a boat that could tip them out into the unforgiving ocean at a moment's notice, and that darkness was impending. But all she could think about was Tex's warmth and the feeling of his muscles through his soaked clothing. She tipped her head back to find that he was bending to kiss her, and captured his mouth with her own.

His hands slid over her salty skin, over her collarbones and down to cup her breasts and pull her closer. He nibbled her neck and caressed her back. If Laura hadn't already been soaked to the skin, she would have become immediately wet.

Tex kissed her again, more demandingly, and one of his hands drifted down her thigh, touching her lightly between the legs.

Laura shifted, inviting him in, and the decking they were on plunged and rocked. Laura clutched at his arm and fumbled her hard-won phone, pulling away with a squeak as she recovered it with a lucky catch.

Bless your reflexes, she told her wolf.

One of us has to be useful, her wolf responded, but it was tinged with affection.

"We should, ah, probably save this thought for later," Laura said breathlessly. "For some time when a good orgasm won't swamp our precarious boat and send us both into the salt."

Tex agreed reluctantly, promising, "I'll save knocking your socks off for when it won't drown us."

Then he noticed, "You have a phone? You brilliant angel!"

"Here's hoping it works," Laura said, touching the button. How she had hated that water proof case when she first put it on.

The screen was so bright it lit them up like a torch, making Laura aware of how quickly that darkness was descending.

"Come on, signal," she said, biting her lip.

"There's a bar! There's a bar!" Tex squeezed her shoulders and they bounced in excitement until the slosh of cool saltwater reminded them how precarious their vessel was. "Can you call your friend at the resort? I don't know the resort's number by memory, but having Bastian come get us will be faster than trying to get the Civil Guard out here to find us. Bastian can tow us back."

With shaking hands, Laura pulled Fred from the contacts and dialed.

It rang, while the sun finished its swandive and its last rays faded at last.

It disconnected without giving Laura a chance to leave a voicemail, and she looked in distress at the low battery warning that popped up. "Let me text him," she said desperately, putting the phone into battery saving mode.

She stalled, looking at the text window. "Lost at sea," she finally typed. "Boat exploded. Contact Bastian."

Her life had certainly taken a surreal turn.

After a moment of thought, she added, "He's the life-guard." She added the emoticon of a dragon impulsively.

The phone registered the text as sent, then viewed, and Laura waited, tensely, for the reply.

Nothing happened.

The bar of signal flickered out and then returned.

She let the screen go to sleep to save the battery life and settled into Tex's careful embrace. The dark water lapped around them, and the bow of the boat dipped and ebbed in the swells that even Laura's night vision could barely make out.

*a*s far as being lost at sea went, Tex thought that things could have been worse.

It was a warm night and they seemed fairly stable on the shard of decking that had survived the explosion. After a short time, the moon, half full, rose to cast a silver-blue sheen over everything.

"I don't think Fred is going to answer," Laura said, puzzled. "I... guess I should call the... what are they called here? Is it 9-1-1?"

"It's 9-1-1," Tex assured her. "And they have an English support line. It's the Civil Guard, they have a coast guard division. Are you sure he saw it? The Mr. Shifter final awards are tonight, so maybe he didn't hear the phone ring."

Laura shrugged under his arm. "The phone says he did. I don't know why it would say he had, if he hadn't." She opened the phone to show him and nearly dropped it as the sliver of boat took an unexpected lurch.

She squeaked and grabbed it hard. Tex watched the line of texts spin backwards as her finger slid across the touchscreen. She started to scroll forward again and slowed down, reading the backchat.

"What is it?" Tex asked, feeling her stiffen.

"This… this conversation. Fred and Jenny." Laura's voice caught in her throat.

Tex tried to guess why it was making her sound so strangled. "Were they having an affair?"

"Ew, no! He was a friend of our dad's! But…"

She let her breath out in a rush and sucked it back in. "He knew that Jenny was planning to use my car and that she wouldn't be at work that morning. She texted and let him know, and he even said he'd be by to pick up a package before she left. I slept through all that… but… he knew. He *knew* I wasn't Jenny. This whole time, he's known I wasn't Jenny."

"That's a little… odd," Tex agreed.

"He could have tampered with my car," Laura said softly. "He's good with electronics, I bet he could have done something to make it go off that curve and look like an accident. He could have rigged at bomb on my laptop, too. And the boat."

Tex had to unclench his fists, consumed with protective rage. "Why would he want you dead?"

Laura gave a hiccup of laughter and shrugged. "He's the closest thing to family we have. Had. I thought we could trust him. I was *this* close to telling him who I was, about a hundred times on this trip. The only reason I hadn't is that I was afraid he would be terrible about keeping a secret, he's so trusting and honest." She snorted. "I guess he was better at keeping secrets than I gave him credit for."

She went rigid again. "My parents… my parents died in a car crash. He was up for the partnership my dad got just a few weeks earlier. You don't think he could have done that?" She sounded shaken to the core.

"I'll find out, if I have to rip off his face to make him talk," Tex snarled, hearing how ridiculous it sounded.

Laura's answering laugh was strained. "Right now, I will settle for solid land under my feet again," she said plaintively. "Gory revenge can wait."

The phone, even though it declared a few percent battery remaining, gave a chirp of protest and shut down. The sudden darkness was stark.

Laura shivered, and Tex wrapped his arms around her, willing more of his warmth into her. He couldn't imagine how it felt, finding out someone she'd trusted had betrayed her.

"I wonder where the otter went," Laura said softly.

"I guess it figured it had done its duty by saving us," Tex shrugged.

There was a streak of light at the horizon and just as Tex was wondering if he'd imagined it, a star of light exploded in the sky above it, followed by a distant boom.

"We're missing the fireworks!" Laura said with a little laugh.

"You kidding?" Tex said, determined to maintain morale. "We have the best seats in the house. From the resort, there'd be palm trees marring up the view. Everyone fighting over the best chairs."

"Jessica Linn would be drunk and bitchy," Laura chuckled. "I'd be sorely tempted to tip her into the pool."

"I think that's an excellent idea," Tex agreed. "Wish I thought of it sooner."

The first fireworks were swiftly followed by more. It was a great show, with swirling white candles and trailing golden globes. A series of red crackers looked a little like a dragon before fading into smoke.

"They'll be having a bonfire on the beach now," Laura said wistfully. "It must be past midnight."

"I'd be set up at the beach bar," Tex said. "And no one would be able to understand that no, I don't have anything on tap there. And no, I didn't haul down the entire collection of single malt scotches. Bastian is probably already out of tiny umbrellas."

"Who do you think won the Mr. World Shifter competition?"

"Mr. Brazil," Tex guessed. "He took the Mr. Speed contest without trouble, and his speech was lovely."

"Nah," Laura said. "He just didn't have the same charisma as some of the others. And Mr. India was a better speaker."

A green shower of sparkles lit up the water in reflections, followed by a rainbow of explosions and a coil of white, sizzling lights.

"Mr. Ireland got the most popular votes," Tex said thoughtfully.

"That will get him the Mr. Internet title, but it won't win him the Mr. Shifter title," Laura said decisively. "His speech went over on the time, so he probably lost points for it. I desperately hope Mr. Canada goes away without placing. I can't believe he won the swimsuit portion."

An amethyst waterfall of spinning lights sparkled off of the waves.

"I wouldn't discount Mr. South Africa," Tex said. "He was in second for the race."

"You were keeping pretty close tabs on these standings," Laura observed wryly.

"It was a little hard to miss what was going on, even if I was being distracted by the hottest thing I'd ever seen in my life," Tex told her.

Laura waited a beat, then teased, "You mean Mr. Brazil, right?"

"I mean, you, you sexy vixen," Tex told her, managing to goose her with one quick arm.

She squeaked and giggled, nearly capsizing them.

They stilled, watching the fireworks continue to dazzle the sky and Laura poked him. "Why haven't you ever sung to me?"

Tex blinked. "Sung to you?"

"Everyone tells me you're a great singer and guitar player, but you've never played me anything." Tex could tell that the whine to her voice was for mostly for show, but he wondered if there wasn't a little real hurt down underneath it.

"I thought you didn't like country music," he said, not entirely truthfully. Really, he cared what she thought and didn't want to be a disappointment to her.

She poked him again. "So sing me something that doesn't have stolen pickups and run-over dogs in it."

Tex cleared his throat, feeling suddenly vulnerable. It was odd not to have his guitar under his fingers. He wracked his brain for an appropriate song, something not too sad or depressing. Finally he chuckled and set a beat on the fiberglass beneath them with his fingers before opening his mouth and singing Johnny Cash's Ring of Fire.

They may not ever be contenders for a reality talent show, Tex thought, but after watching the backstage of the Mr. World Shifter contest, he wasn't sure he'd ever do that kind of thing anyway.

For the moment, this was perfect, singing only for his mate. Laura was finally relaxed next to him and Tex was singing the last few repeats of the ring of fire, not wanting to break the spell, before he recognized that one of the blaze of fireworks... wasn't fireworks at all.

"That's Bastian," he said, with sudden relief, pointing.

Something dark was flying near the surface of the water, periodically lighting the area with flame. The finale of the fireworks, a chaotic, brilliant, flower garden of light, lit up the top of its wings. It was obviously a dragon, skimming just above the water in a search pattern.

CHAPTER 25

$\mathcal{S}$he was adrift on an unsteady piece of a blown-up boat, in a dark ocean with non-sequitur fireworks exploding overhead and Tex was singing Johnny Cash to her. Laura felt like she was caught up in a crazy analogy of her own crazy life.

When Tex stood up, waving his hands and shouting to attract Bastian's attention, the shard of boat jerked alarmingly. Laura squeaked and tried to flatten herself further, stabilizing their makeshift craft. Warm water splashed over the surface of the decking, soaking parts of her clothing that had only just gotten dry.

But it worked. Within a few moments, Bastian caught sight of Tex, or heard his ridiculous cowboy yodeling, and circled around to fly straight for them. He dove into the water just in front of their craft and came out of the water in human form, pulling himself partway up and asking flippantly, "Hey, you guys need some help?"

Swamped in the water that rushed up over the decking due to his extra weight, Laura could only laugh weakly. "I'd love a drink."

Bastian tsked. "What kind of bartender are you, Tex, coming out all this way on a romantic excursion with no drinks?"

Tex, crouching again to keep them from capsizing, mock laughed. "Very funny, Bastian. All the booze sank with the boat. Can you tow us home?"

Bastian was already inspecting what was left of the railing and nodded in approval. "Shouldn't be a problem." He had a little coil of rope unclipped from his belt and began tying a sturdy knot. "The real problem," he added, "is what Scarlet it going to say when she sees what you did to her boat."

"It won't compare to what she'll say when she realizes the entire shipment of wine is at the bottom of the drink," Tex said.

"How did you know to come looking for us?" Laura had to ask. "Did Fred tell you?" Something was very wrong with the entire situation with Fred and she had a bone-deep need to understand it, as badly as she didn't want to believe it.

"Fred? That balding fellow with the nervous twitch? No, he hasn't had anything to say beyond asking for more drinks at the bar. Which by the way, Tex, I don't think Scarlet is ever going to let you leave again. No one can keep the natives from getting restless like you can. No, it was an otter that clued me in."

"An otter?" said Tex and Laura together in aston-ishment.

"We were just talking about whether I should go out after you when it came right up on the beach looking utterly wiped out, dragging what was left of your hat. Must have swum it's little heart out, poor thing."

Twice that otter had saved them, Laura realized, and she felt unsettled.

"Now, speaking of swimming a heart out, you two hold on. I can move a little faster than an otter."

Bastian shifted as he dove back into the water, jeweled scales cutting through the waves in the pale moonlight like diamonds. He had the other end of the rope in his mouth, and Laura was glad that she'd taken his advice to heart and wrapped both arms around a piece of railing.

The rope went taut with a jerk and they were gliding across the water like a poor attempt at a water skate, every other wave cresting over and drenching them. Laura was pathetically grateful when Tex wiggled his way over to her and reached around so he was cradling her between his arms as he held them both on.

She even felt safe enough to take some enjoyment out of the wild ride; the water seemed to be going past as fast as it did on the boat, but they were down at the surface of it. It felt like they were part of it, like they were somehow connected to the ocean's fierce energy.

It was difficult to look up, as that meant a faceful of water periodically, but glances showed Laura first a glimmer of light on the horizon, then it resolved into the familiar terraces of Shifting Sands, the pool deck lit like a beacon. There was a dying bonfire on the beach.

Over the reef, the water was suddenly much more still, and Laura could look up and see all the gorgeous levels of the resort. It felt like home and she suspected that not all of the saltwater on her face was from the ocean.

Bastian remained in dragon shape as they got to the beach and pulled the boat fragment far up onto the sand. A few remaining guests and tired staff reached hands to help them up from the fiberglass shard.

Laura was wrapped in a thick towel and handed a bottle of water.

She was stiff from the long wait in the cool night air

and her whole body protested the workout that had come from holding herself in place while being dragged back to shore.

Everyone had questions and Laura truthfully answered what she could, not bringing Fred into the conversation but keeping a wary eye out for him in the crowd.

Tex was never far from her side and she was glad to lean on him.

"Your hat," Bastian said, handing Tex what was left of it.

"It's all chewed up," he said mournfully. "I've had that hat for fifteen years!"

"Give the otter a break," Laura said, feeling defensive of the creature who had been so good to them. "What happened to it? The otter, I mean."

"Gizelle wrapped it up in a towel and took it up to the pool deck," Bastian said. "Muttering about her human being scared, too, and something about long swims and water that wasn't wet. You know Gizelle. About half of it is nonsense."

"And half of it isn't," Tex said thoughtfully, fingering the hole in his hat.

Laura swayed on her feet as a wave of exhaustion broke over her and Bastian immediately noticed. "You guys have been through a lot. Do you want some dinner?"

"Breakfast, actually," said Breck, indicating the dawn breaking on the horizon.

Laura's stomach rumbled distinctly, but she said, "A shower. I'd really like a shower first."

The crowd dispersed, back to their drinks and what was left of the bonfire, and let Tex and Laura climb the stairs from the beach up to the pool deck alone.

CHAPTER 26

*T*ex was not surprised to find Scarlet waiting for them at the top of the stairs, her critical gaze taking careful stock of their condition. Gizelle was sitting cross-legged on one of the lounge chairs, a towel cradled in her arms. The sunrise was gaining strength and casting glowing orange light over the white deck.

"I presume the boat was lost," Scarlet said without preamble.

"Bastian dragged the biggest piece back, but I'm afraid it's not terribly seaworthy," Tex told her, too tired to be intimidated by her non-nonsense air. "Everything was lost."

"Except you, I'm glad to see" Scarlet said gently, her nod including Laura. "Insurance will cover the rest. I presume it was not merely an... accident."

At Tex's side, Laura suddenly went stiff and Tex looked around to see Fred, standing at the foot of the stairs from the bar deck.

They were both watching him when he caught sight of

them and the expression of disbelief and anger was so brief that Tex actually doubted he'd seen it.

Laura had no such doubts.

"If you want answers," she told Scarlet furiously, "ask him!"

Fred managed to look innocent and slightly offended at the same time. "What do you mean, Jenny? Are you okay? What happened?"

"What I don't understand," Laura said, voice heartbroken, "is why. Why would you try to hurt Jenny? Why would you try to hurt *me*? What did we ever do to you?"

Tex was still watching Fred's face, held back from roaring across the tile to smash the man into the ground only by Laura's hand on his arm.

For just a moment, Fred looked shocked and angry, but it was so swiftly masked in hurt innocence that Tex might have been fooled if he hadn't been watching for any sign of guilt.

Before he could do more than growl, there was a streak of fur and the otter that Gizelle had been holding bolted towards Fred, shrieking in fury.

Fred stepped back, nearly tripping on the first step up to the bar deck.

The otter chittered and growled and seemed bigger than an otter ought to be.

Gizelle dashed after the creature and knelt a short space away from it, gazing intently at it. "Use your words," she scolded gently. "Remember yourself!" She ignored Fred completely.

Tex was still trying to figure out how to attack Fred without stepping on the otter or mauling Gizelle on his way when the otter shimmered, seemed to hiccup in form.

It was the most painful shift that Tex had ever witnessed, as if otter and human were fighting for control of the form. Fur stretched, limbs took unnatural shapes and lengths one at a time. Finally, it became...

"Laura?"

He had to check to see that Laura was still standing at his side, mouth open in shock.

"Jenny!"

Then his mate was leaping into the chaos, weeping and throwing her arms around a mirror image of herself.

"You're not dead, I couldn't feel you anymore, I thought you were gone."

"Couldn't," Jenny said, awkwardly. She was swaying, as if exhausted and not sure how her own limbs worked. She picked up a hand, which Tex realized still had short webbed fingers and claws and inspected it thoughtfully. "Lost."

Gizelle looked at Laura warningly. "She's not very found yet," she said.

Tex was not looking at Fred anymore, captured by the drama unfolding.

"I'm not sure if this simplifies or complicates matters," Scarlet said mildly at his elbow.

Fred turned as if to flee and Tex caught the motion out of the corner of his eye. He moved without thinking, crossing the space between them and grabbing him by the back of the neck. His bear wanted to crush the loathsome man, bite his windpipe, and maul his smug face, but Tex reined him back, satisfying his blood lust with a simple shake that left Fred gasping for breath.

Laura wrapped her towel around Jenny's naked shoulders and drew her to one of the lounge chairs. "What happened?"

"She needed help," Jenny answered, in a sing-song voice that Tex knew wasn't hers. "I saw a place for me."

"Was it Fred?" Laura asked, desperately. "Did he booby-trap my car so that you got hurt?"

Jenny cocked her head at her. "Booby-trap?" She considered. "Yes. And another car, long ago."

Laura sucked her breath in. "Our parents?"

"They had things he want. Things he valued. Money?"

"There was no money," Laura scoffed. "We were paupers."

"There was!" Jenny said, more strongly now, more like Laura would have, Tex thought.

It was very disconcerting, seeing two of them together, features so familiar and dear. It was even more disconcerting watching Jenny struggle with her otter companion.

"What happened to it?" Laura asked, incredulously.

Jenny seemed to rally herself. "Fred very carefully managed it away for us, so it looked like it was just bled away on the market, or lost to taxes, but it was really going into his accounts. And he didn't tell us about the life insurance at all. But I caught him and I figured out what he'd done."

"Your laptop. He blew up your laptop after he saw that I'd accessed your accounts."

Laura's mirror nodded firmly. "He'd do that," she agreed.

"And the boat," Laura said, "He blew up the boat after I told him that I had everything I needed on the cloud. I was just talking nonsense, but he thought I'd figured out what you had figured out and was going to expose him."

"I had enough on him to send him jail for a very long time and we would have been very rich indeed. Mom and Dad's life insurance policy alone would have set us both up for life. We were millionaires, Laura. We just didn't know it."

With a moan, Jenny's eyes rolled up into her head and she slowly shifted into an otter who took two wobbly steps and fell at Laura's feet.

CHAPTER 27

*J*enny was alive! She was real, and whole, at least in body, and she was somehow now a shifter. What's more, they were apparently much richer than Laura had ever realized was possible. She gathered the dazed little otter up and cradled her gently. "Are you okay?" she asked plaintively. How cruel would it be to get her sister back, just to lose her so soon?

Gizelle stepped forward with the towel she had the otter wrapped in previously. "There isn't much room in one mind," she said cryptically. "But your sister is still there."

"I won't let him get away with any of it," Laura promised her armful of unconscious otter, wrapping the towel gently around it.

Tex gave Fred another shake, only needing one arm and a grip at the back of his neck to make him plead for mercy.

"Enough!" Fred croaked.

Laura could only imagine the restraint that Tex was showing, given the fury on his expressive face.

She could relate!

"I loved your Dad like a brother," Fred explained to Tex sullenly. "But he got everything that should have been mine. He was a shifter, I wasn't. He got your Mom. He got two beautiful daughters. He got the partnership at the firm. Sure, I got rid of them, but I raised you two like you were my own after that, or I would have, if you hadn't gone haring off after high school. I set Jenny up at our firm when she graduated, and her thanks for that was getting a partnership offer that should have been mine."

"If they offered her a partnership, Jenny earned it," Laura snarled.

Fred ignored her, continuing his confession. "I knew that she was onto the insurance money before I got her text that she was going to be bailing you out again. I thought I could get her out of the way, and do with Laura what I'd failed to do with Jenny. She would confess her masquerade once it got hard to maintain, and I'd protect her and *she'd* be the grateful daughter I deserved."

"Then why did you try to poison me with rattlesnake venom?" Laura demanded. "This is not the way to earn a daughter's love, not that any of this was."

Fred spread his hands innocently, and this innocence was more believable than his earlier show. "I had nothing to do with that. I didn't try to hurt you until you gave me no choice."

Laura didn't want to believe him, but the latte was such a different attempt than the others that Fred had confessed to. And however twisted his motives, he had followed them.

"Where would I even get rattlesnake venom?" he asked. "It's not like they sell it in the gift shop!"

"Then who did?" Tex growled. Laura could tell that it was taking all of his self-control not to flatten the odious man.

"It was probably my cousin," said a new voice. Laura turned to see the man in sunglasses from the mainland bazaar she'd overheard mentioning Shifting Sands. He was walking up the steps from the beach with Bastian.

"Who are you?" Scarlet, Tex, and Laura asked together.

"I saw you on the mainland asking questions about the resort," Laura added suspiciously.

Bastion explained, "He pulled up in a boat and demanded to see Scarlet."

"My name is Sid," the stranger explained, and his smile showed fangs that were just a little sharper and longer than they should have been. "My cousin Maryanne works here. I've come to bring her home."

"Who the hell is Maryanne?" Laura asked incredulously. "And why should she want to poison *me*?"

"We don't have a Maryanne on the staff," Scarlet said with a frown.

Sid ran tired fingers through his hair. "She's probably under an assumed name. She's... not entirely right in the head. She has a habit of lying about who she is, fabricating these involved personas to be, fixating on people who are kind to her. She's a rattlesnake shifter, which makes her little fantasies especially dangerous if they get disturbed."

"Marie," Tex said, in a strangled voice. "Marie thought I was her hero." It was hard for Laura to blame her. He was the best-looking guy at the resort, during a world male beauty pageant, and he was sweet and gentle and perfect.

Scarlet frowned. "She said she was a genet. From France."

"We're from Arizona. She's been missing from the home she's supposed to be in for about six weeks and needs to be on her medication again," Sid said apologetically.

"I'm really sorry for the trouble, I hope you weren't hurt, ma'am."

"I wasn't," Laura assured him, still mystified.

"You have some kind of proof of this?" Scarlet asked. "I am unlikely to release a member of my staff to a stranger on the weight of one person's word."

"I have paperwork from her doctor," Sid assured her. "I can give you the number of her facility."

"Please take her," a familiar voice begged.

Laura looked at the side entrance of the pool deck to find that Juan Lopez was approaching, looking wild-eyed and nervous as he came through the arch of greenery. "She's completely nuts! I can't get her to leave me alone! Ever since I put that damned fire out, she's following me around with goo-goo eyes, talking about destiny and heroes."

Laura smirked. It couldn't have happened to a more deserving jerk.

Scarlet was rubbing the bridge of her nose. "Well, this certainly explains everything, even if it does introduce some new complications." She gave Sid a hard look. "Presuming your paperwork checks out, I will release Marie—Maryanne—to your custody."

"Thank you, ma'am," Sid said humbly. "I would, ah, appreciate it if we could leave the authorities out of things. She forgets that she's venomous, sometimes, and doesn't understand consequences."

"There is a report on file with the civil guard for the initial incident," Scarlet said candidly. "But they tend to turn a blind eye to what happens out here. If they pursue an investigation, I shall simply tell them that it turned out to be a... misunderstanding."

Sid nodded. "I think that's an accurate summary," he said wryly. "She really doesn't understand what she's doing."

Scarlet was already turning away from him. "You, on the other hand," she said in icy tones to Fred. "You are a problem."

Fred was glaring sullenly at the ground. Tex helpfully tipped his head up. "It's good manners to look at a lady who's talking to you. I could escort him off the resort," he offered suggestively.

"As tempting as it is to walk him off the cliffs, we *will* let the civil guard deal with *him*. I'm sure he'll be extradited to the US for his crimes there."

Tex looked disappointed, but brightened when Scarlet suggested, "Truss him up in the meantime. I don't take attempts on my staff's life lightly."

Laura wasn't sure when she had gone from guest to staff, but hearing Scarlet say it let a knot of tension unravel in her chest.

"Juan? Juan darling?" Marie's—Maryanne's—false French accent was light and airy above the island sounds of surf and rustling leaves. "Where aaaare you?"

Juan groaned and bolted for the stairs. "You haven't seen me!" he shouted as he fled.

Maryanne did a double-take when she walked through the side door. "Sid!" she cried.

"I'm here to take you home, Maryanne."

Maryanne pouted artistically. "But I was having so much fun!"

"You almost killed someone!" Sid protested. "Again!"

"She didn't get hurt," Maryanne whined. "It was all just pretend."

Sid rubbed the bridge of his nose, much as Scarlet had earlier. "I told you that you can't spit in people's coffee. It's bad! Let's go home, kitten. I'll help you pack up."

"Oo," said Maryanne. "I'll show you my room!" Her

French accent was completely gone. She took Sid's hand willingly and tripped off with him towards the staff housing.

CHAPTER 28

ex growled at Fred to stay and cowed him enough to obey while he ducked into the pool's mechanical room and found the duct tape. "I'm afraid all we have on hand is pink duct tape," he said without apology.

Fred gave a token struggle as Tex trussed up his wrists, thought about it, and did his ankles, too.

"Hey, I've got rights," Fred protested. "This isn't constitutional! You can't leave me like this!"

"We're not in the US," Tex reminded him. "But you're right, I can't leave you like that." Another piece of duct tape went over Fred's mouth and Laura laughed out loud.

"That will do," Scarlet said, not disapprovingly. "I'll send Graham down to watch him." She turned away from his wiggling protests to address Laura. "You are, of course, welcome to stay as long as you need. Your sister will need some time and help to come to terms with being a shifter and this is a safe place to do that."

"I can work," Laura said automatically. "I'm happy to help at the spa, or make beds, or do laundry."

"We can come to an arrangement in a day or two," Scarlet suggested. "Get a good night's—a good morning's sleep. Eat and have a shower. Gizelle can watch over Jenny while you rest."

Gizelle bobbed her head up and down vigorously and stepped forward to take the little bundle. "I won't let the darkness burn her," she promised.

Laura gave her a quizzical look, then reluctantly passed her the towel-wrapped otter.

As Gizelle trotted off to... wherever it was that Gizelle stayed at night, Scarlet frowned at Tex. "You head to bed, too. We'll be seeing most of our guests off today and everyone will get a little well-deserved break." She strode off up the stairs towards the restaurant.

Tex suspected Scarlet would not be getting any immediate rest herself.

"Well, handsome," Laura told Tex, "Let's go to bed. You made certain suggestive promises on what was left of the boat that I expect you to make good on."

Tex tried to tip his hat to her and his fingers found the otter-chewed hole. "I could find the energy for that," he agreed as they slowly climbed the stairs, heading without consulting each other towards Tex's room in the staff house.

"We'll get you a new hat," Laura promised. "Jenny said we're millionaires, remember?"

"I thought you hated the hat," Tex said. "This would be your chance to get rid of it."

"It's grown on me," Laura decided. "And you wouldn't be you without it."

"I wouldn't be me without you," Tex told her, stopping on the stairs to look her earnestly in the face. "Everything else is just trappings."

"I love you, Tex," Laura told him solemnly. "I love all

the parts that make you, even the big belt buckle and the beat up hat. I want you to sing me the saddest, countriest songs you know, because you love them and I love you."

Tex's slow, earthy smile was as brilliant as the sun in the tropical sky. "I love you, Laurelangelina Lily."

"Fancy you remembering that whole name," Laura said, clearly impressed.

Tex moved closer. "I also remember that promise I made you about knocking your socks off when we were safe on land."

"I'm not wearing socks," Laura told him suggestively.

"I'll improvise," Tex promised.

EPILOGUE

*L*aura tossed her sandals to one side and settled into the nearest beach chair. Tex was restocking the little self-serve beach cabana and cleaning up the ravages of the party from the night before. The late afternoon beach was all theirs, empty lounge chairs and beach umbrellas invitingly lonely. The piece of the boat they'd been stranded on still lay at one end near the dock, a few crabs enjoying the rare afternoon shade beneath it.

"Everything's sorted," Laura said with great relief.

Tex closed the little cooler and walked over to pick up one of her feet to rub. "Did you talk to Tony?"

Laura nodded, letting his clever fingers massage her toes. She'd been on the phone for nearly three hours with the operative of a mysterious government agency that represented shifter issues. It didn't sound like hard work, but she'd spent most of the call pacing nervously.

"He's got all the paperwork in motion for getting me declared not dead," she said. "We're going with the story that I was concussed, picked up by an illegal Central American fisher, and eventually left here at the resort. Fred has been transferred to American custody already. Our testimony might not have been enough, but he had rambled an insane confession before they even made the exchange with the Civil Guard. Tony says that it's going to take a while to unravel the paperwork regarding the inheritance, but signs are good that the money will be ours free and clear."

"And the cartel?"

"He took my testimony and got the slow grinding gears of the American legal system working on that, as well. He thinks it's a good idea that Jenny and I lay low here until they've gathered enough evidence, which is probably best for a while anyway."

"How *is* Jenny?" Tex asked, more seriously, switching feet.

"Oo," Laura said, as his fingers found the sorest spots. "She's... better. Shifting is still really painful for her, and she hasn't exactly sorted out how to deal with the otter in her head, but Gizelle says she can help her."

"I'm so glad you have her back," Tex said, in his sincere drawl.

"Me, too," Laura agreed. She took her feet back and sat up, looking up towards the pool deck. "The resort seems so peaceful today," she said wonderingly.

"This is a lot more normal for us," Tex assured her sitting beside her and putting an arm over her shoulders. "Last week was an anomaly, and while it looks like we've got more business than usual coming up, by comparison, it should be pretty quiet."

"I am going to love working here," Laura said with a sigh, letting Tex nibble at her neck.

"Scarlet would probably let you stay on credit," Tex told her.

Laura shook her head. "I don't want to," she said

firmly. "Even if we're millionaires or whatever, I think I'd rather be part of something like this than sit on my ass paying people to wait on me."

"It's a fine ass," Tex said admiringly.

"Undeniably," Laura teased back. "I hope you'll have time to finally play that guitar you drag everywhere, now that it's quieter."

It was leaning in the beach cabana now, and it didn't take more than the suggestion for Tex to walk over and get it. He sat back down with it cradle in his hands, testing the tuning with a few bars of a Spanish love song.

Laura leaned back and let him start playing a sad song about death that took a bizarre turn halfway through and turned into a plea to prop his corpse up by the jukebox if he died.

Laura ended up in tears of laughter and clapped as he played the final lines. "All these years I thought I hated country music," she said, "and didn't realize what I was missing."

Then she sobered. "There is something terribly important I am still missing though."

Tex looked worried and his fingers, which had continued playing chords, stilled on the strings. "What is it? Anything you need, I'll get it for you."

"I never found out who won the Mr. Shifter competition," Laura told him with deadpan seriousness. "My life cannot be complete without this knowledge!"

The lines around Tex's eyes crinkled perfectly with his laugh. "Mr. India," he told her, when his guffaws let him. "Mr. Brazil was the first runner up and Mr. Ireland was the second runner up. Did you lose any bets?"

Laura shrugged. "I'm just tickled that Mr. Canada didn't place. That was my only desire."

"Your only desire?" Tex said suggestively. He kissed her neck again, letting teeth brush her skin.

"Well, maybe not my *only* desire," Laura agreed with a breathless laugh.

They made it back to Laura's little cottage in the jungle with their clothing barely intact; Tex had gotten his shirt off, and Laura's shorts were unbuttoned by the time the door was open. The remaining articles had been shed by the time they reached the bed.

Tex lowered her onto the mattress as if she were weightless, then joined her there, his skin like hot velvet against hers.

He paused, thick member at her entrance, but not pressing. "I'm yours," he told her, voice low and rough with emotion.

Wild with need and hunger, Laura pressed herself up and around him. "I'm yours," she agreed.

But Tex held back. "Do you mean it?" he asked.

Laura stilled. "I mean it completely," she said. "I'm *yours.*"

Tex nuzzled her, then nibbled at the place where her shoulder met neck as he entered her.

Her cry was all pleasure, and she arched up to his strong thrust. "Oh, yes…"

Tex claimed his mate with every stroke and touch, bound to the lush woman as he'd never imagined was possible. "I'm yours," he told her, between ragged breaths.

"I know," she told him.

∾

TEX'S COCKTAIL RECIPES

Shifter's Mate

Ingredients:

1 1/2 oz Light rum

1/2 oz cas juice (aka sour guava.)

1/2 oz Orange curaçao

1/2 oz Orgeat syrup

3/4 oz Dark rum (Centanario)

Preparation:

Shake first four items together in a cocktail shaker with ice. Strain into glass with fresh ice and float dark rum on top. Garnish with cubes of fruit and an umbrella, serve with a straw.

∾

Rise and Shine

Ingredients:

8 oz Iced coffee

1/2 oz Orange curaçao
Whipped Cream

Preparation:
Mix first two ingredients, serve in tall mug over ice with garnish of orange and whipped cream.

≈

The Hairy Martini

Ingredients:
    1/2 oz dry vermouth
    3 oz gin
    1/2 oz kiwi syrup

Preparation:
Mix all ingredients in cocktail shaker with ice. Strain into glass (straight) or over ice (on the rocks). Garnish with a kiwi slice with the skin still on. Umbrella optional.

≈

Magnolia's Mango Mojito

Ingredients:
    2 oz Light rum
    generous fistful of mint leaves
    4 oz mango juice
    1 teaspoon of superfine sugar

Preparation:
Bruise the mint leaves in the rum, stir in sugar and

mango juice until sugar is dissolved. Serve over crushed ice and garnish with fresh mint and a wedge of lime.

Graham's Ginger Snap

Ingredients:
    1 1/2 oz vodka
    1 oz ginger liqueur
    1 oz fresh lemon juice
    1/4 teaspoon agave syrup
    1/4 teaspoon grated fresh ginger
    Pinch cinnamon
    Pinch cloves
    Pinch nutmeg

Preparation:
    Shake all ingredients in a cocktail mixer. Serve over ice with a cinnamon stick.

A NOTE FROM ZOE CHANT

I hope you enjoyed Tex and Laura's book! Thank you so much for reading it!

I always love to know what you thought – you can leave a review at Amazon or Goodreads (I read every one, and they help other readers find me, too!) or email me at zoechantebooks@gmail.com.

If you'd like to be emailed when I release my next book, please click here to be added to my mailing list. You can also visit my webpage, or follow me on Facebook. You are also invited to join my VIP Readers Group on Facebook, where I show off new covers first, and you can get sneak previews and ask questions.

Keep reading for a preview chapter from the next book in the Shifting Sands Resort series, *Tropical Lynx's Lover*, where we follow Jenny's journey to making peace with her otter… and finding her mate!

WRITING AS ELVA BIRCH

A Day Care for Shifters: A hot new full-length series about adorable shifter kids and their struggling single parents in a town full of mystery and surprise. Start the series with Wolf's Instinct, when Addison comes to Nickel City to take a job at a very special day care and finds a family to belong to. Funny and full of feeling, this is a gentle ice-cream-straight-from-the-container escape. Sweet and sizzling!

~

The Royal Dragons of Alaska: A fascinating alternate world where Alaska is ruled by secret dragon shifters. Adventure, romance, and humor! Reluctant royalty, relentless enemies… dogs, camping, and magic! Start with The Dragon Prince of Alaska.

~

Suddenly Shifters: A hilarious series of novellas, serials, and shorts set in the small town of Anders Canyon, where something (in the water?) is making ordinary citizens turn into shifters. Start with Something in the Water! Also available in audio!

~

Lawn Ornament Shifters: The series that was only supposed to be a joke, this is a collection of short, ridiculous romances featuring unusual shifters, myths, and magic. Cross-your-legs funny and full of heart! Start with The Flamingo's Fated Mate!

～

Birch Hearts: An enchanting collection of short stories and novellas. Unconstrained by theme or setting, each short read has romance, magic, and heart, with a satisfying conclusion. And always, the impossible and irresistible. Start with a sampler plate in Prompted 2 for fourteen pieces of sweet-to-sizzling flash fiction, or the novella, Better Half. Breakup is a free story!

MORE FROM ZOE CHANT

Shifting Sands Resort: A complete ten-book series - plus two collections of shorts. This is a sizzling shifter romance set at a tropical island resort. Each book stands alone but connects into a great mystery with a thrilling conclusion. Start with Tropical Tiger Spy or dive in to the Omnibus edition, with all of the novels, short stories, and novellas in my preferred reading order! Shifting Sands Resort crosses over with Shifter Kingdom and Fire and Rescue Shifters.

∼

Fae Shifter Knights: A complete four-book fantasy portal romp, with cute pets and swoon-worthy knights stuck in a world of wonders like refrigerators and ham sandwiches. Start with Dragon of Glass!

∼

Green Valley Shifters: A sweet, small town series with single dads, secret shifters, sweet kids, and spinsters. Low-peril and steamy! Standalone books where you can revisit your favorite characters - this series is also complete with six books! Start with Dancing Bearfoot! This series crosses over with **Virtue Shifters**, which starts with Timber Wolf.

SUPPORT ME ON PATREON

What is Patreon?

Patreon is a site where readers and fans can support creators with monthly subscriptions.

At my Patreon, I have tiers with early rough drafts of my books, flash fiction, coloring pages, signed and sketched paperbacks, exclusive swag, original artwork, photographs…and so much more! Every month is a little different, and there is a price for every budget. Patreon allows me to do projects that aren't very commercial and makes my income stream a little less unpredictable. It also gives me a place to connect with my fans!

Come find out what's going on behind the scenes and keep me creating at Patreon! patreon.com/ellenmillion

TROPICAL LYNX'S LOVER: SNEAK PREVIEW

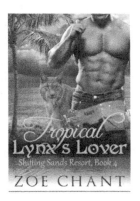

Jennavivianna Smith wasn't floating.

For the first time in a very long time, she wasn't floating.

She wasn't all-Jenny, yet, but she wasn't as not-Jenny as she had been, and she kept her eyes screwed shut for a while after she was actually awake, trying to process what had happened.

"You're not sleeping anymore!"

At first, Jenny thought that it was her own thoughts.

Her own, weirdly divided thoughts. The otter inside her that wasn't her, but was, all at once.

"You can't fool me," the voice said firmly, and Jenny remembered.

She remembered Gizelle, the slight, salt-and-pepper-haired woman who had talked her back into human form, and remembered seeing Fred again and feeling the sting of his betrayal, and Laura, oh, Laura! Her twin was there in her head again, that unspoken connection they'd always had was back and as strong and comforting as it had always been, even when they were at odds, or miles apart.

She opened her eyes. She was in a little square of neat lawn near a white gravel path, tall, flowering jungle brush on all sides. She could hear the ocean, and smell it's sharp, salty tang, but she couldn't see anything past the dense foliage.

Gizelle was kneeling above her, hair wild around her face, big eyes earnest. "Come on, then, you've had a good sleep."

Jenny opened her mouth to protest that the sleep had been restless, and full of floating dreams, but it came out as half-trill and half-purr, and she snapped otter jaws together again.

"It takes a little while, that's all. Come and walk on two legs with me. See your sister!"

Jenny balked. The last time she had changed from otter to human, it had burned. She remembered the feeling of her bones cracking and resetting, the muscles stretching impossibly, the tendons snapping into new places.

"Don't be afraid," Gizelle said coaxingly.

"Don't baby me," Jenny wanted to tell her, but couldn't, through otter teeth. Nothing frustrated her more than being patronized.

Don't act like a baby, then, her otter told her. Its voice in her head was not scornful, exactly, but teasing, prodding.

Jenny felt more stung than she knew she ought to. *I'm not being a baby.*

Of course you aren't, her otter mocked. *You're a 'grown-up' coward.*

With an otter sigh of frustration, Jenny stretched.

At first, it was simply a stretch of otter limbs, then Jenny focused furiously, remembering human arms and human legs, and she reached and wrenched herself back into her own form.

Gizelle clapped her hands in delight as Jenny lay on the ground, naked and panting. "Good job!" she said enthusiastically.

"Don't baby me," Jenny was finally able to say, breathlessly.

Then don't-

Shut up. Jenny was dismayed to see that her fingers were still slightly webbed, and tipped with sharp claws. She ran her tongue over teeth that were too sharp and grimaced.

Gizelle took no notice of Jenny's crabbiness, simply offering her hands to stand up.

Let's go run around on those human legs you love so much, her otter suggested. *Maybe go swimming at the beach.*

I'm a little naked, Jenny reminded her, accepting Gizelle's offered hands and climbing to her feet.

I know, her otter purred back at her, full of mischief. Images of admiring men accompanied the rejoinder. Jenny felt her skin heat, hating herself for how the idea stirred in her loins.

"How do you do this?" Jenny demanded of Gizelle, standing unsteadily.

"I know, it's weird there's only two of them," Gizelle said comfortingly.

"Only two?" Jenny asked. Were there shifters with more than one extra voice?

"You just have to shift your weight between each one, and not think about it too much to keep your balance."

When Jenny looked blankly at her, Gizelle scampered away and ran in a circle. "Like this!" she called merrily.

"You meant *legs*," Jenny realized. "Only two *legs*."

Returning, Gizelle said, "Of course I meant *legs*. What else would I mean?"

"I thought you meant voices," Jenny said, feeling foolish.

"There are always more than two voices," Gizelle said solemnly, eyes big in her face.

Jenny had just started feeling like things made sense, and then suddenly she didn't again. She could feel her otter's amusement, and shunted it away. "There's more?" she said unhappily. She could barely stand otter's demanding voice, should she expect more of them?

"Voices that whisper. Voices in the sky with no sun. Feathered voices. Voices that—"

"Gizelle," said a new voice, gently chiding.

Jenny turned, half-crouching, and nearly let her otter take control of her skin again instinctively. *No!* she thought fiercely, fighting to stay in human skin.

The red-haired woman from the night before stood at the opening in the hedge by the white path. She was neatly dressed, and Jenny was relieved to see that she was holding a summery dress.

It was her own dress, Jenny realized, and more memories flooded back. Laura, her twin, had come to the resort pretending to be Jenny, and of course she would have packed Jenny's clothing for the trip.

Naked would be more fun, her otter pouted at her.

Jenny ignored the voice.

"I'm Scarlet," the woman said, handing her the dress and looking politely aside while Jenny struggled to put it on. "I run Shifting Sands."

Jenny, still trying to work out how to get her head through the neckhole and feeling stumped by the armholes, was keenly aware of Gizelle staring at her.

"Gizelle," Scarlet said kindly.

"She's really bad at that," Gizelle said frankly.

"I need you to help Graham in the upper gardens, please." Scarlet's tone made it sound less like a request and more like a royal command.

Triumphant at last over the openings in the dress, Jenny pulled it fiercely down over her generous curves.

"Bye!" said Gizelle merrily, and she skipped off across the lawn and out the way Scarlet had come. Her footsteps were quiet on the gravel, and Jenny realized she was barefoot.

"I apologize for Gizelle," Scarlet said, sounding not the slightest bit apologetic. "She has taken great interest in you."

"She's not neurotypical, is she," Jenny observed. It felt ironic to say so, since she felt so much less than normal herself.

Normal is boring, her otter told her.

"We released Gizelle from a madman's prison less than a year ago and it took her a long time to shift from her gazelle form," Scarlet explained. "She remembers nothing about her life in his zoo. We have no idea how old she is, or where she came from before then. She may even have been born there." She gave Jenny an intense, appraising look. "How much do *you* remember?"

Jenny gazed back at Scarlet without seeing her. "I remember driving. It was Laura's car, I was just going to get her a few things from the supermarket. There was an explosion—I lost control of the car, and it went off a curve. I remember going through the guardrail…"

She shuddered, remembering the scream of metal and the drop into the shattering ocean below, hitting her head, waves and water and sinking…

Comfort came from an unexpected source.

I caught you. I was there for you.

Jenny pushed back. She didn't want to be grateful to the interloper in her head.

"I shifted," she said woodenly. "I've never shifted before. I didn't know I could. I don't think I could, before."

Scarlet listened, but offered no comment.

Jenny worked her mouth, trying to find words for what came next. She had been more otter than herself, eating, swimming, floating in sleep. She was drawn south, swimming earnestly, day after day, through currents that became gradually warmer.

"I found Laura after her boat exploded. I didn't really think about things, only knew that I had to help her, and where I could find that help."

"Shifting Sands was always meant to be a safe haven for shifters," Scarlet said, nodding.

Jenny felt her eyebrows scrunch together. "Shifting… Sands. I worked on the contract for this place." Life before this seemed impossibly distant and long ago. "I was—I am —a lawyer."

"What else do you remember?" Scarlet asked gently.

"I remember Fred," Jenny said firmly. "He betrayed us. He was the one who sabotaged Laura's car, and her boat. And… our parents. He killed our parents, so long ago." Somehow, it stung as much now as it had when Jenny had first uncovered the treachery, weeks ago.

"He's in custody," Scarlet promised fiercely. "He will never be able to hurt you again."

Jenny tried to take comfort in the idea, and nodded.

Somewhere, far away, there was a beep of a horn and shouting voices, and Scarlet frowned. "Let me take you to the dining hall. You've missed lunch, but there's a buffet available and you must be hungry after your long ordeal."

On cue, Jenny's stomach rumbled, and she and her otter finally agreed on something.

"I'm famished," she admitted. Then she added, "Just please, tell me I don't have to eat raw fish or urchins for a long, long time."

She didn't think she would ever enjoy a sushi bar again.

Click to read the rest of *Tropical Lynx's Lover*!